barely
hanging
on

Also by Karen Rivers

Waiting to Dive

The Actual Total Truth

Karen Rivers

barely
hanging
on

Cover photo by Rodrigo Moreno

Originally published as *The Gold Diggers Club*

Scholastic Canada Ltd.
Toronto New York London Auckland Sydney
Mexico City New Delhi Hong Kong Buenos Aires

Scholastic Canada Ltd.
604 King Street West, Toronto, Ontario M5V 1E1, Canada

Scholastic Inc.
557 Broadway, New York, NY 10012, USA

Scholastic Australia Pty Limited
PO Box 579, Gosford, NSW 2250, Australia

Scholastic New Zealand Limited
Private Bag 94407, Greenmount, Auckland, New Zealand

Scholastic Children's Books
Euston House, 24 Eversholt Street,
London NW1 1DB, UK

*The author wishes to acknowledge the support of
the Canada Council for the Arts.*

 Canada Council   Conseil des Arts
for the Arts   du Canada

Library and Archives Canada Cataloguing in Publication

Rivers, Karen, 1970-
[Gold diggers club]
Barely hanging on / Karen Rivers.

Previously published under title: The gold diggers club.
ISBN 978-0-439-93825-9

I. Title. II. Title: Gold diggers club.

PS8585.I8778G64 2007   jC813'.54   C2006-906675-2

6 5 4 3 2 1   Printed in Canada   07 08 09 10 11

*To everyone who ever hunted for gold and
ended up finding something better along the way.
And to Mum and Dad, for the island,
with all its hidden treasures.*

— K.R.

chapter 1

This has started out to be practically the worst day in the world. I'm not kidding. For one thing, last night I had the most horrible dream ever. It was about my mum. My mum is having a baby. In real life, not just in the dream. The baby won't come until July, and it's only February. I *know* that, okay? But in dream-time that doesn't make any difference. In the dream she was having the baby, like today. Her belly was huge, bigger than a basketball or a beachball or any kind of ball. I mean it. It was enormous. In real life, it is still just a tiny bulge, but in the dream she was gigantic. She looked barely like a person! Particularly considering that she had very small, beady eyes, like rat's eyes or something even more awful than that. If I were going to be honest here, I'd say she didn't look much like my mum at all, more like an especially large and unfriendly rodent. Somehow I knew it was my mum though, in the way that you know things in dreams. Which was weird because my mum is really very pretty. I don't look anything like her. She has long blond hair and perfect teeth. My hair isn't blond and my teeth are very small and spaced apart. They look like the teeth of a much smaller person or a baby. It isn't good. I don't even think they can fix the kind of teeth that I have, unless there are some kind of braces that make your teeth bigger.

Anyway, in the dream I was shivering cold (probably my window was open in real life; I like the window open when I sleep so that I can breathe fresh air) and there was snow all around. We were walking through a big field and there was no one else there and it was really creepily quiet. I could hear the snow crunching under our shoes. I only sort of knew it was a dream, if you know what I mean. It did snow yesterday, so the whole snow thing made it feel kind of real. Then all of a sudden Mum-monster said, "Oh Carly, your sister's coming," and out of her snowsuit popped this fully grown little girl the same size as me, only she had skin like a snake and her eyes were red and flashing. I screamed and screamed. I mean, I really did scream. I screamed so loud that I came out of the dream and woke up and I was standing on my bed and Mum and my New Dad were standing there staring at me like I was some kind of alien creature. Me! Huh. I tried to explain to them about the dream, but dreams are hard to tell to other people. They never sound as scary when you say them out loud, and sometimes they sound even a little bit funny. I could see my mum try not to laugh a bit when I got to the part about the lizard skin. Really. That isn't very nice, I'm sure you'll agree.

Dad (I call him Dad, even though he isn't my Real Dad) made me some hot soy milk and stayed up with me for a little while, but he couldn't stop yawning. Mum fell asleep on my bed. She snores. This isn't her prettiest quality, I can tell you that. I hope I don't snore, but how would I know for sure? Finally Dad went back to bed in his own room. I turned off the light, but all the shadows started to look like the Reptile Girl, so I turned it back on. Mum didn't wake up, which is good, because she is very grouchy when she gets woken up unexpectedly. Luckily, she can sleep through almost anything. She says that her body is making a baby and it uses up a lot of energy, so she needs her rest. I suppose that must be true.

I can't imagine why she wants another baby. After all, she has me. I'm Carly. I'm ten going on eleven. By the time this baby is my age, I'll be twenty-one! I'll be an adult. I'll be old enough to have kids of my own! And she'll just be a kid. Or he. Whatever. Also, as far as kids go, my mum has Marly, who is five, and Shane, who is almost three. That seems like more than enough, even though Marly and Shane aren't really hers. They came with my New Dad. A complete package. The only thing he didn't bring along was a dog, which is good because we already have two dogs. We have Roo, who was my Real Dad's dog, and I have a dog of my very own called Blue. The rhyming names were a joke. Like Carly and Marly. Which is also a joke, but not that funny.

My full name is Carly Abbott-Fitzgerald. The Fitzgerald is new. On Christmas I told my New Dad that I would take his last name. It sounds kind of weird, but my last name was Abbott and when Mum married my New Dad, she took his name, which is Fitzgerald, but I didn't want to do that. People called me that because they didn't know, or whatever, but I didn't change it officially. I mean, I already had a perfectly good name. My Real Dad's name. He died, but that doesn't change anything. I was the only one in the family with a different name. Then all of a sudden I decided I didn't always want to be the different one, so I tacked the Fitzgerald onto the end of my name. Who knew you could do that? Now I'm Carly Abbott-Fitzgerald on paper. It was totally a big deal, but really it's quite meaningless. I mean, in real life I'm still just me, Carly. Nothing is different. My new name is quite a bit more glamorous than the real me. I like it though. Perhaps I will grow into it. It sounds like the name of a movie star or a super-model or even a gold-medal-winning athlete.

My mum snored all the rest of the night and I couldn't get back to sleep, so I read a book for an hour or two and then my alarm went off. The book was *Little Women*, in case you were wondering. It is both good and not good. I get tired of the way they are always dressing up and fussing with their hair and blah, blah, blah, but I like to read it. I like Jo. She is tough and I imagine if it had been an option for her at the time, she would have enjoyed diving as much as I do.

I should tell you that I'm hoping to be an Olympic diver when I grow up. Probably by the time my new sister/brother is my age, in fact. That's kind of neat to think about. I didn't realize that until just now. I'll have to remember to tell Mum that later. I'm sure she'll be excited. What she has thought of (and tells everyone who asks) is that I'll be just the right age to babysit the new baby for free. Ha! That's funny. If I'm going to be babysitting anyone, I will demand to be paid. A lot. I don't babysit Marly and Shane because I'm too young. You have to be twelve to babysit for some reason. Not that I would want to look after those two. That would be a handful, I'm sure. I barely like spending the weekend with them, to tell you the honest truth. They are just here on weekends most of the time, because they have a mother and she has them the rest of the time. We have them for all this month, though, because their mother is away in Australia, which I am quite jealous about. Who goes to Australia? It is a million miles away from here. I want to go to Australia very badly. I've seen it on TV and it looks very nice and hot and the animals are much more interesting than ours and also there are a lot of terrific divers from Australia. The Olympics were there once. There is a lot of money there for sports, or so Dad tells me.

It is now sometime in the afternoon and I am at school and I'm tired and frankly I'm in no mood for today. Also, not being able to sleep has affected my hair and it is sticking out all over the place and little wisps of it keep floating by my eyes to remind me how gross it is. I feel ugly and mad. So there. And today is a stupid day. Do you want to know what day it is? Well, you can guess. It's the stupidest day of the year.

Yes indeedy, it's stupid *Valentine's* Day. Yuck.

I don't know who invented such a stupid day, but my teacher, whose name is Mrs. Whitfield (although I like to call her Mrs. Witless because she has no sense of humour whatsoever and is always yelling at me), decided that everyone had to make a stupid valentine for another person in the class, and that person had to be someone who was not your friend. For example, if you are a girl, the card has to be for a boy. You can imagine how much fun this is, can't you? So I made my stupid card, and I gave it to this boy named Tim because I think he is cute. A bit cute, not a lot. He dives with me in the Dolphin Diving Club. He is pretty good, but not that good. I used to think he was pretty good. I should say, used to, as in, not anymore. I also used to think he was cute. Now I know he is not cute or even slightly nice.

This is what happened: I made a nice, beautiful card with hearts made of tissue paper and very delicate little Kleenex flowers and . . . I kid you not . . . he opened it and laughed at it and held it up to the light. It was a little wispy, I grant you that, because it was so *delicate*. And then he BLEW HIS NOSE ON IT. He says he thought it was a Kleenex.

I am so mad that I could spit. To make it even worse, the only boy who gave me a valentine was this weird kid named Smith. Smith has braces and his hair is so white it is almost non-existent. From a distance it is the same colour as his white skin, so it just looks like a bald head. Baldness freaks me out. His card was very nice, though. Very artistic and also funny. Not that it makes it less humiliating to get a card from him. I mean, really. Smith!

And to make it even worse, that stupid Tim, who I *used* to think was cute, made a big red and purple card for my best friend Montana. Montana got six cards. Huh! What am I supposed to think? I love Montana. And I mean love in the way that you love your family kind of love. Not girl-boy kind of love. Duh. Obviously. Montana is my best friend in the world, but sometimes I hate her a little bit because she is totally beautiful. She is beautiful *and* nice *and* smart *and* brave. Something horrible happened last year, which I will tell you quickly so that you know, if you don't know already.

It happened when we were diving off rocks at my cabin. My cabin is on an island near here, but to get there you have to take a boat. Sometimes I am allowed to bring friends, and on this weekend

I was allowed to bring two friends because Mealy Marly and Shane were away. So me and Montana and Sam (my best friend from diving club) were practising our dives into the water, which was dark and blackish-green. Well, not really. It was just regular water, but when you stood on the rock and looked in, it looked like it was green. You couldn't see the bottom. I guess there was stuff down there that we didn't know about. Obviously. How could we have known? Montana dove into a sunken log and broke her back. It was super scary, in a very bad way. When I tell it quickly, it doesn't seem so bad, but trust me, it was. To make it worse, when she was in the hospital, they cut off all her hair. Which you would think would make her less perfectly gorgeous. But instead she now has it in a really cute pixie cut and she looks better than ever. Really, I'm very happy about it. I am. She is almost completely patched up from the accident, although she doesn't dive anymore because part of her back doesn't bend — it has a steel rod in it — and sometimes she gets tired faster than the rest of us, but she is almost back to her normal self. I don't want you to think I am a horrible person for being a tiny bit jealous about the valentines. Actually, I'm not jealous at all, I've decided. After all, who wants a stupid valentine from stupid Tim, the Nose Blower?

Not that I care, but Felicia, who is our other friend in this class, got three cards. She is not perfectly gorgeous like Montana but she is funny and smart. What is wrong with me? I am just Little Miss Unpopular. I don't know why. I'm a nice girl! I smile at people! Mum always says it doesn't matter what you look like, as long as you smile a lot. I do smile a lot. I find a lot of things funny, for Pete's sake. All that smiling should have got me at least two cards. Oh, forget it. Obviously, I am repellant to boys and will spend the rest of my life alone. That's just fine because I am a very busy person and don't have time to worry about boys and all that other stuff. I have a lot going on. On Saturdays and Wednesdays, I have diving practice first thing in the morning, at, like, six o'clock. It is very important to get up at the very crack of dawn to practise, because then you feel like you are really sacrificing something for your sport. In this case, the sacrifice is sleeping. I'm all for sleeping, but I'd rather dive. Besides, when I get famous they will do a TV show about me and I need to be able to say how early I used to get up, and Mum and Dad will need to talk about how they never had to wake me because I was always awake because I was so excited about practice. This isn't always entirely true, but I will coach them to say it on the TV special, when there is one.

So you see that I am very busy. Also, I take gymnastics after school on Tuesdays and Fridays. On Wednesdays, I take my not-really-my-sister Marly to piano lessons and then take her home to her mum's house on the bus. My mum says this is a good experience for me with responsibility, but the truth is that she works until four o'clock on Wednesdays and Dad works until five. So you can see how this works. I can do this not-so-fun job, but I can't babysit for money. Whatever. I like the bus. I always meet super-interesting people on the bus. Once I met a man who claimed to be Jesus Christ. I don't think he really was. Well, clearly, he wasn't. But he looked the part, what with the beard and wild hair.

On Mondays, I play at Montana's house, or Felicia's house, or Sam's house. I only tell you all this so you see how full my weeks are. I have no time for boys! I don't care about valentines. Not at all. I glare at Smith until he blushes, which is about ten seconds because he has thinner skin than me and blushes very easily. I feel a little bit mean, but I don't care because I'm in a bad mood. If I grow up and marry Smith we will have pale children with bad hair, which cannot happen. I feel bad about glaring but the sooner he knows, the better. I don't want this to get out of hand.

I decide to spend the rest of the afternoon carving my name into my desk with the compass from my geometry set. The compass, I'm sure you'll agree, isn't good for much else, except for drawing perfect circles. But only if you want to draw a circle with a hole in the middle. One thing that works to avoid this is to stick the pin part in an eraser first and then spin it around while it is stuck in the eraser. It is harder to make a perfect circle this way though, because the eraser sometimes moves. Well, you try it. You'll see what I mean.

I'm very good at carving on my desk without getting caught. It's an art, as Dad would say. He says everything is an art, when it clearly isn't. I don't get it, but I say it all the time. I can't help it. He must influence me more than he thinks. I carve all through Science and partway into Math, which was the second-to-last class of the day, when something horribly embarrassing happens. I don't even want to tell you what.

Oh, forget it. I'll just tell you then, and you'll laugh and laugh, but it isn't funny and it hurt. Okay. Don't read this if you don't like gory stories! Don't say I didn't warn you!

I was carving away, very quietly — *scrape,*

scrape, scrape — when the compass *slipped from my hand* and I *stabbed* it into the fat part of my other hand at the bottom of my thumb. Not gently, either. I was working on the curlicue part at the bottom of the *y* of my name. I was pressing quite hard! The stupid compass skidded and jammed into my thumb and got stuck. To be honest, I might have screamed. At least, I mumbled, "Help! Help!" Finally someone noticed, and Mrs. Whitfield came over and pulled it out and there was a big sploosh of blood and I *fainted*. I'm not kidding. First she was there, and then the room went all grey and the next thing I knew I was opening my eyes and my head was hanging upside down and everyone was staring at me.

I'll probably never live this down.

I have to get a shot, like right away, so that I don't get tetanus, which is a fatal and terrible disease. The shot hurts also, but not as much as the whole compass situation. I wonder if that's what it feels like to pierce your ears. If so, I'm sure I don't want anything to do with it. I'm allowed to get my ears pierced when I am eleven, which is coming up soon, so this is something I've been thinking about a great deal.

After the shot, I lie down in the nurse's room for several minutes and contemplate my total humiliation. It is quite possible that I will die of embarrassment if I have to go back to class. I decide that I will stay here in the nurse's room until after school, and then I will sneak quietly away. This is a great room. The nurse is very nice and lets me do an eye test and a hearing test. I pass both of those much more easily than I pass most tests. She also lets me take my temperature and stuff. This is fun. Well, it isn't really fun, but it's much better than going back to class.

"You have a lovely office," I tell her. I am trying to have an adult conversation.

"Uh, thanks," she says. She keeps looking at the phone. When it rings, she practically leaps on it. She must have a very interesting life, and the phone call is probably from her gorgeous boyfriend. She giggles a bit into the phone, which is somewhat disconcerting. I mean, she's the nurse. I can tell she doesn't want me to listen, so I go look out her window. This office has big windows, and it is a nice-ish day outside because it snowed yesterday and today it is sunny, so everything looks very bright and clean and fresh. Probably the snow is melting though, and what looks nice and fresh from here is actually slush. I hate slush. It is the absolute worst. It is useless for snowballs and snowmen and does not crunch under your feet like proper snow. It has no point. It is just like very wet, very cold puddles. I have to walk home today, too, which is not nice. I should get rides at least on days when it snows. It hardly ever snows here. Once or twice a year at the most. The snow-fall yesterday was quite a surprise. I took the kids outside and we made snow forts. It was perfect building snow. Not today. Like I said, today it's just slush and *blech.*

The nurse is on the phone for ages and I'm getting bored. This day is not improving. I hate to imagine what else will happen. So far, there has been the Valentine Fiasco and the Compass Stabbing. When she finally hangs up, I lie down on the green vinyl couch and start asking questions. Her name is Stephanie and she is from Quebec. I have never met anyone from Quebec before. She says she speaks French but she has no accent at all. She says people speak both languages in Quebec, and she spoke mostly English. I'm not sure that could be true. Sometimes I watch the French channel and it is all French, all the time. I don't understand a word of it. Which is funny, because I do speak a bit of French. Well, not really. I can say, "Where is the bathroom?" (*"Où est la salle de bain?"*) but that's about all. Finally, after an hour, she says, "Carly, I think you'll be just fine, you should probably head back." Secretly, I think she is just annoyed by my questions. I am very interested in other people, and sometimes I ask them too much and they get short with me. Stephanie was getting a little short, so I knew it was over.

So I go back to class.

I take the long way, up the stairs and down the other stairs and around the outside bike racks — there are only about ten bikes because who rides their bike in the snow? — and back through the door by the gym where the little kids are playing some weird game that involves flags and balls. It looks kind of fun, so I watch through the window for a while, and then I realize that it's freezing outside and I don't have a jacket. I wish I did, because then I could stay out here for longer, but I'm cold as anything so I go in.

I slide into my seat and I'm blushing like mad, so I keep my head down. I blush easily, though not as easily as Smith. I like to think that I blush "prettily." Amy is always "blushing prettily" in *Little Women*. I guess this is a situation where anyone would blush. Montana passes me a note that says, *Are you okay?* I just nod really fast and I don't look at her because I feel so stupid. I try to concentrate on what Mrs. Whitfield is blah, blah, blahing about, and it turns out she is assigning us a project to do in groups of three about something historical that happened around here, such as the Gold Rush or whatever. We can pick what we want to do, but we have to write a paper and do a presentation about it. Yuck! Horrible-ness!

We get to talk about our project for the last fifteen minutes of school, so naturally my "group" will be Montana and Felicia and instead of talking about *that* we talk about what it felt like to pass out and I let them peek under my Band-Aid at the hole made by the stupid compass and I show them the mark from the needle. We giggle about the valentines for a bit and finally the bell goes and it's time to go home.

It's Tuesday, so I only get to go home for an hour and have something to eat such as fruit or raw vegetables, and then I go to gymnastics. I would much prefer to have a cookie or some cake or something but my mum is a health-food freak suddenly. Particularly since she got pregnant. I'm lucky to get granola on a good day. It takes about ten minutes to walk home, and the slush is wet and soaks into my pants. My mood is bad. Basically I am very, very mad because the day was so horrible, so I am stomping into puddles and getting mud all over myself. Which makes me madder. I don't care. I'm sure I'll get in trouble and that will just cap off this day to perfection.

I get home and try the door and it's locked, which is wonderful because I don't have a key. Who locks their own kid out of the house? This is insane! I have to go to the bathroom so badly I will probably pee my pants. How could the house be locked? This is a horrible, crazy joke, clearly. I ring the doorbell and the dogs bark so I talk to them through the glass, but no one opens it.

"Roo," I say. "Let me in!" She kind of barks again in a howly sort of way and paws the glass blocks on her side. That's all very well, but it doesn't open the door.

Where could they all be? I go look for the car in the driveway and it isn't there. Immediately, I get to feeling a little worried. Maybe it isn't Tuesday, maybe it's Monday and I'm supposed to be some-where else. Have I got it all mixed up? I'm only ten; I'm much too young to start forgetting things. Mum forgets things sometimes; she says it's "pregnant brain," which means, I guess, that pregnancy makes you forgetful. Maybe she forgot that today was Tuesday and went somewhere, accidentally thinking that I was going somewhere else. I don't know quite what to do. I could try to climb in a window, but I can't open them. A win-dow up high is open a bit, but I can't see how I can reach it without a ladder. We don't have a ladder.

I sit on the stoop, which is covered with a bit of wet, half-melted snow. It's very, very cold as it seeps slowly through my pants, but I'm too upset to move. It looks like I wet my pants, which I didn't, although I'm not far from it. I put my head in my hands. I'm practising making my super-annoyed face so that when Mum pulls into the driveway and is all apologetic and stuff then I can pretend to be really mad instead of relieved, which frankly I would be if she showed up. I'm going to be late for gymnastics and won't have time to eat my celery or whatever today's treat might be.

I am there for maybe ten minutes when Mr. Taft from across the street comes running over. I can see his face and I start to feel really panicky, like I might faint again, because he has this really alarmed look.

"Carly!" he says, "I'm sorry, I was planning to be here to let you in!"

This is very weird, because I've barely ever talked to him and he's never let me into my own house before. So I say, "Why's that?"

And he says, "It's your mum, Carly, she had to go to the hospital, it's the baby." And I swear, I just about faint again. I sit down really hard and probably bruise my bottom very badly and tears come to my eyes, but I'm not really crying.

He says very quickly, "She's fine though, it's okay, Carly, really, she's fine, she wanted me to tell you that she'll be home in an hour and it was a false alarm. Carly, don't cry!" He kind of half-hugs me and pulls me upright and takes me inside, and he makes me the most delicious hot chocolate I've ever had. I didn't even know we had the stuff for hot chocolate. Is this soy? It's amazing. It tastes like hot, melted chocolate ice cream. And finally, I start to calm down a little bit and I tell him about fainting at school. He's very funny about it and makes me giggle. I never knew he was funny. He was just Mr. Taft-with-the-perfect-lawn before. Now I know much more about him. For instance, he used to be a professional golfer. He was on TV. He played all over the world and won money if he played well. If he didn't, he didn't get paid. Now he teaches golf at the golf course up the street. He lights up when he talks about golf. He must love it like I love diving. Perhaps that's why his lawn is so perfect — it's like a golf course. He is going to teach me to play golf one day, maybe, if I have time. I tell him I have a lot of other stuff going on, such as diving and so on, and may not ever have time. But he doesn't seem that upset. Really, he is very nice about it.

Finally, after an hour or more, I hear the car in

the driveway and I start to feel scared again, so I run out to meet Mum and Dad. They have Marly and Shane with them, which seems a little unfair as I have been home by myself and worried sick and they are all happy and not worried. It isn't fair. But I don't even make a Big Deal of it because I'm so happy to see Mum and Dad. Usually, I am happy to make a Big Deal when it comes to Mealy Marly and Shane. Today, I am almost glad to see them. Well, not really.

I get snow and slush all over my bare feet, which is kind of fun, particularly seeing as I can go right back inside and warm them up. There are hugs all around and we all pile into the kitchen. Mr. Taft goes home. Mum tells me that she just had a tummyache and thought it was something to do with the baby. Well I guess it was, in a way, and what it means is that she has to stop working, for one thing. She is an appliance salesperson, in that she sells fridges and stoves and so on and is on her feet all day. But no more of that! She has to lie down a lot until the baby is born, and some person named Nanny is going to move into our house for a while and work here full-time helping out and stuff. This is also good news because there is always the possibility that this Nanny will cook things like hamburgers and fried chicken which we normally would never get to eat unless they were made of tofu. Maybe Nanny will also be nicer than Mum, who I don't mind telling you is turning into a bit of a grouch. The bad part of it is that the new room that Dad built downstairs, which was going to be my new room when the baby comes, will be this Nanny's room while she is living with us. That isn't fair, but I can see this isn't a good time to argue about it, and I'm just happy Mum's okay.

Fine, that isn't true, the truth is that I said, "But that's my room, she can't have my room!"

And Mum said, "It's just for a little while."

And I said, "No way!" And then I said, "I hate you and this stupid baby!" I just added that last part for a dramatic flair. I didn't mean for it to be so, well, mean.

And then Mum said, "Carly, for God's sake, I really don't want to deal with this kind of nonsense from you right now."

"Why not?" I said. "Because it's something about me for a change and not about the stupid new baby."

And she started to say something, but instead she kind of made a coughing sound and *burst into tears*. Of course, I felt horrible, so I said that this Nanny-person could have my room after all and that it was fine. It isn't really fine. I was looking forward to that room. I was going to paint the walls this super pale purple colour that I had already picked out. Also, it is bigger than my current room. We were going to choose the carpet this weekend. But I hate seeing my mum cry. There is nothing worse. I guess that she had a pretty bad day and didn't need for me to make it worse. So I let it go. See, I can be nice, right?

But I'm still mad about the room.

We end up ordering a pizza and watching movies, which is something that never happens on a school night. I miss gymnastics altogether, but Mum says that's okay because tonight is a special family night where we get to celebrate that we're a family and that my little brother/sister is okay. It's not that much of a celebration because Marly gets a stomach ache from eating cheese and starts having a big, huge temper tantrum. Shane tries to hug her to make it better and she pushes him and he nearly falls down the stairs. Those two can be really annoying. My stomach kind of hurts, too, because I'm not used to eating things that taste like anything other than cardboard. But you don't see me pushing anyone down the stairs, do you?

And that is the end of my horrible, stupid day.

chapter 2

"Carly, c'mon, stop fooling around," Montana says.

"Stop fooling around, Miss Abbott-Fitzgerald!" I say, mimicking Mrs. Witless, which makes Montana laugh. Mrs. Witless has a very strange accent. It is a bit British, which is interesting because I asked and she has never been to Britain. I don't know why so many people in this town have fake British accents. It makes no sense. They call this place "A Little Bit of Olde England," which is embarrassing at best. But I still don't know how you could get an accent out of that.

"Seriously, Carly, we have to figure this out," Montana says. "We only have a month to do this project!"

"We will," I tell her. "In a sec." Clearly, she does not realize that a month is a very long time.

"A month," Felicia says, laughing. "We have ages."

In case you are wondering what we are doing, me and Montana and Felicia are downstairs in my house in the Other Room. We call it the Other Room because it is a room with no name. Like, it's not a bedroom or a living room or a dining room or a den. It's just a room. There is a trapeze in the middle of it hanging from the ceiling, and I'm doing some somersaults on it because it's fun, not because I am showing off. Okay, possibly I'm showing off just a little. There isn't much else in the Other Room apart from the trapeze and some bookshelves stuffed with Dad's books and an old beanbag chair and a computer desk with the computer on it. There is another computer upstairs but this one is "for the kids," which means me, because the other kids are too young for the computer or don't care about it. The floor is made of cement which is painted in a bunch of different colours all swirled together. It was supposed to be fun and artistic, but it looks like puke. My mum did it during a "Martha" moment. She saw something on TV, and Dad said, "Uh-oh, I sense a Martha moment coming on!" And she swatted him with a rolled-up magazine. Anyway, it didn't stop her. She rushed right out to the paint store and next thing you know there is paint in multicolours glopped all over the floor. It was not as "lovely" or easy as she thought, I guess. It looks like what would happen if you fed Roo a big vat of different-coloured ice cream and she barfed. I'm sure you can imagine it. We covered most of it up with a big green rug, although the big green rug is not a picture of loveliness either.

"Can I have a turn?" Felicia says, eyeing the trapeze. She is a guest, so I get off and let her try. I hope she doesn't fall. She isn't very sporty. She is clever, but not athletic. Anyway, she kind of gets one leg stuck, and I'm laughing like crazy at her antics, and I realize that Montana is ignoring us and reading a book from the shelf.

"What are you doing?" I ask, irritably. She is always doing the "right" thing, and in this case the "right" thing is to be working on the project, so I'm sure she is doing something smart. I'm still a bit annoyed with her regarding the valentine she got from Tim. Or at least, I would be if I still thought he was a bit cute. "We haven't decided what our project is going to be about yet."

"Carly," she says. "This is great!" She holds up the book and starts waving it around so we can't see what it is.

"Argh!" I yell and grab it out of her hands. It is a little weird-looking book called *Canada's False*

Prophet, The Notorious Brother XII.

Brother XII! I know about him because at the cabin last summer Dad was telling us that Brother XII was a crazy old coot and that he hid gold all over the place. In fact, Montana and Sam and Felicia and me made up a club — the Gold Diggers Club! — and we were going to look for the gold this summer. I don't know that I want to do a project about it though. It's kind of a private thing, not something I want to tell the whole entire class about. Really. I mean, what if someone else catches on to the idea and they all go racing up to my cabin and start digging for treasures? What a nightmare! I can think of nothing worse than looking down the hill from our lovely deck and seeing Tim the Nose Blower trudging along with a treasure map and a shovel. Also, the book doesn't look that great to me. It is ugly and small and smells of dust. It has no pictures. There are many better books on the shelf. My favourite is a big one called *Sharks, Whales and Dolphins.* It has many beautiful photographs. Marine biology is quite interesting. If the diving thing doesn't work out for me, I might consider marine biology — although I am very terrified of sharks.

"What's so great about it?" asks Felicia, holding the book away from her nose and sneezing not once, not twice, but five times in a row without stopping.

"For our project," says Montana. "Duh. It's perfect!"

"What's so perfect about it?" I ask.

"Carly," she says. "Don't you remember? Your dad was telling us last year when we were at the cabin. About Brother XII. And the gold that he hid! And his weird cult or whatever. It's historical, right?"

"I guess," I say. "But that's a thing that we are just going to do, it doesn't have to be our project. I mean . . . I just . . . "

"And it's local . . . " Felicia says, her eyes brightening.

"I guess," I say.

"So?" says Montana. "We can do the research now *and* get the project done *and* figure out where to find the gold at the cabin this summer!"

"Oh, all right," I agree. I'm reluctant. I mean, seriously, we don't want to tell the whole world about this treasure, do we?

"Yay!" says Felicia. "Now we should take a break and do something else."

"No way," says Montana in a voice that means business. "We have work to do!"

Really, her enthusiasm for schoolwork is very

annoying sometimes. I stick out my tongue, but she ignores me so I get to work looking for other books and stuff. Yes, about Brother XII. There are three books altogether, which is perfect because there are three of us. I take the one with pictures. I mean, it's hard to get interested in someone unless you can see what they look like. This Brother XII looks like an old teacher or something. He has a pointy little beard. I wouldn't say that he was crazy just from the look of him. He doesn't look half as crazy as that guy Jesus that I met on the bus.

There is only one picture of him, and a bunch of other pictures of cabins and whatnot on the island. Which is a little bit interesting, but not totally. Okay, it is fun to see pictures of the island with all these houses on it. Their cabins were very nice, almost nicer than ours. They were made of logs and really looked more like proper houses than cabins. I try to start reading, but my thoughts aren't really concentrating. To tell you the truth, I don't much understand most of it. Well, any of it. It's all about Egyptian symbols and some weird religion and a big court case, as far as I can tell. Not much about gold. Secretly, I think our project might be more interesting if we wrote about, say, the Gold Rush, or something like that.

But I don't say anything. I kind of feel like this

should have been my idea and not Montana's because after all, it is my cabin. Brother XII is kind of mine, too, in a weird sort of way. You know what I mean.

I get to work making the backboard for our presentation even though Montana gets a bit huffy because we haven't done any of the work part yet. "Don't worry," I tell her. "We'll just paint the title. It will probably inspire us."

Pretty soon, we have accomplished next to nothing, but we have a big blue placard that says *The Notorious (and Crazy!) Brother XII's Treasure!* at the top, and it's time for Montana and Felicia to go home. The "crazy" part was my idea. If we just called it "The Notorious Brother XII" it would mean that we basically just copied the title of the book. And that would be cheating or something, I'm sure. Also, to make it interesting, we have to talk mostly about the treasure, particularly when you consider we don't understand the other stuff. And Mrs. Witless is always yacking on about putting things in our *own* words. The girls are each going to take home a book to read and take notes from it for the project. Before Montana can assign us too much homework, I hear the shoes of all the adults above us in the kitchen, tromping around. Thank goodness. All that reading and work was giving me a headache.

After they're gone, I take my assigned book upstairs and lie down on my bed to read it, but pretty soon I'm not reading it at all, I'm just staring at the page and thinking about diving tomorrow and about my last diving practice.

Nothing much happened that was out of the ordinary, except this one thing that I'm trying to figure out, and that is that Tim (the Nose Blower) came up to me at the end of practice and said, "Nice diving today!" in this really jolly way, which seemed odd. And then he said, "My mum says I have to thank you for the card." And then he kind of giggled and ran away. I don't think I like the idea that everyone in his family knows that I made him a valentine and that he blew his nose on it. I mean, please. That is totally, horribly embarrassing, isn't it? He did look a bit sorry, though, and he was nice about my diving, which wasn't very good that day, to tell you the truth.

I am learning to do dives from the platform and, frankly, I think it is very, very scary. Not as scary as sharks or ghosts, but close. My friend Sam loves it, so I pretend to love it too. Ha. I'm sure she can tell that I'm shaking like a leaf the whole time. She just runs out there and dives off it like it's just the springboard, which it isn't. For one thing, it doesn't spring; for another, it is about a hundred miles up. I can't do much of a dive from there, and she can do some pretty fancy stuff. She is incredibly brave and tough. I'm just a wimp. Honestly. I hate that about myself. Why am I afraid? I'm not afraid on the other board and it is pretty high. Well, okay, it's not. It's three metres high, and is my favourite one. But it is nothing like the big old concrete platform tower. I blame this on my mother. I mean, obviously she never took me up to high places when I was a little kid and so I'm not used to them. I used to climb trees, but that isn't quite like this.

This is what happens. I climb up to the top of the ladder and all those tiny stairs. Well, it is all sort of stairs in that there are wider foot parts and they are at an angle like stairs. They aren't actual stairs, though they are very steep. You wouldn't want to fall. By the time I get up there, it is all I can do to walk down to the end and sort of fall off it in a dive-like way without fainting from fear. Each time I do it, it feels brand new, like I've never done it before. My heart stops beating altogether, I'm sure of it. Then there is just the whistling sound in my ears of all that air rushing by and then the *swack* of the water. The board itself is quite wide, which is good, and feels very solid under my feet, but that doesn't seem to help that much. To be honest, I'm a little worried, what with the fainting that happened last week at school. What if I faint when I'm up there? Would anyone notice? Would I fall off the edge? Just thinking about falling off the edge makes my knees wobble and I'm lying on my bed, for Pete's sake. I force myself to close my eyes and imagine climbing up there and not being afraid and doing a regular dive and not falling. I do it over and over again in my head until I feel less nervous, and when I open my eyes again it's dinnertime! Yippee!

Now, normally I'm not so excited about dinner, but things are different because now that Jenny cooks for us (her name is Jenny, not Nanny as I originally thought, duh) we have really good food. It isn't burgers and pizza, but she makes the most delicious stir-fry type things that are often spicy. I like her because she talks to me like I'm a grown-up and she isn't always snapping at me like Mum is. She tells me that Mum is just tired and cranky because of her huge belly and because she isn't always feeling well. Jenny is so nice. She is also very pretty and has a boyfriend named Grant who is handsome and smart and goes to university where he is studying to be a doctor. My friend Montana might be a doctor when she grows up, too. She can't be a diver like me because of her back. That's okay, though, because being a doctor is very important and may even be better than being a diver.

Maybe when my diving career is over, like when I'm twenty-five or something, maybe then I'll be a doctor. I doubt it though. It is more likely that I will do something like teaching diving, like my instructor Jon.

Tonight Mr. Taft is over for dinner. Mum says that it is to thank him for looking after me when I was freaking out. I resent that. I wasn't totally freaking out; I was just a tiny bit concerned, that's all. When I get downstairs, he is already there and Dad is pouring him a glass of milk and saying, "Trust me, you'll need this!" And they are all chortling in the way that adults laugh at something they aren't sure is funny.

Dad has taken to drinking milk with dinner because he gets heartburn. I've never had heartburn and I'm sure I don't want it, so I'm drinking milk, too. And it's real milk (organic), not soy milk, because Mum read somewhere that soy milk has something in it that I've never heard of that may or may not be bad and she doesn't want to risk hurting the baby. Now that Mum isn't working, she has lots of time to read. She must have learned by now that everything might either be good for you or not good for you, because she seems to have given up a bit on the whole crazy tofu kick she was on. It could be that she is just tired, though, or maybe being pregnant makes you crave spicy stir-fries like this one. She is certainly tucking into it tonight. I stare at her as she shovels food into her mouth.

"I'm eating for two," she says, and winks at me.

She says that a lot. She better watch out or she will get as big as the Mum-monster in my dream.

Other than reading, Mum also has lots of time to get involved with my life in a big, huge way. So as soon as I start to eat, she gets right to badgering me about the project, what is it, what am I doing for it, who is doing what, and blah-de-blah-de-blah.

"It's about Brother XII," I said. "Don't worry about it!"

"But which part are you doing?" she asks.

"Mum," I say. "Really. I've been doing my own homework for a long time now. You don't need to get involved."

"Carly," says Dad. "Don't be rude to your mother."

"What?" I say, truly outraged. "I'm not being rude."

"Carly," says my mum in her I'm-about-to-get-mad voice. "I do think you are being a little bit rude."

"Oh, fine," I say. "It's about stupid Brother XII, who did goodness knows what, with a bunch of people, who came from all over the place to the island where the cabin is, and they built houses and then burned them down and left. Nothing about gold," I add, glaring at Dad, who put the idea in my head to begin with.

"Ah," Mr. Taft says, "Brother XII and the gold. Do you want to hear what I know about it?"

"Not particularly," I say meanly, slurping up some chicken and peppers. "What do you know about it anyway?" Honestly, I don't know why I am so nasty sometimes. I just get this feeling like I'm really irritated and I can't help myself. I roll my eyes at him for good measure. He doesn't see me, so I do it for Jenny, who giggles a little bit and then shakes her finger at me. I'm getting very good at the eye-rolling. The other day Mum said to me, "Goodness Carly, you're starting to act like a teenager." I'm sure she didn't mean it as a compliment but I said thank you anyway.

"Well," Mr. Taft says, "My grandfather was one of Brother XII's followers."

"What?" I say, leaning forward. After all, this could perhaps be interesting. Even better than that, if he knows something about it then maybe I won't have to read any more of these dull, weird books.

"Oh, so now you're interested," he says in a funny way and then he looks at my dad and they laugh like that was something super-funny to say.

I don't know how much I like this Mr. Taft anymore, to tell you the truth.

"Forget it," I tell him. "I don't want to know. I can just read it in a book. It's not a big deal, anyway. I mean it's a Grade Five project. It's not, like, rocket science or something."

"I'm kind of interested," Mum says. Which is good, because I kind of am as well. "Really, Gary, that is quite fascinating to think you have a connection to this story." Gary. Ha ha ha! What a name!

"Okay," says Dad. "Why don't you tell us, but not Carly. I don't want her to have to hear this *boring* story."

"Whatever," I mumble.

"Well," Mr. Taft (Gary!) starts. "My grandfather was an astrologist and lived in California . . . "

Right away I stop paying attention and start thinking about California. Now, I've never been to California, although I have been to Hawaii, which was very nice. California has Disneyland, of course, and all kinds of other places like that, and I'm thinking that I would like to go there. Of course, seeing as I am a wimp and am afraid of heights, I probably would freak out on all the rides and embarrass myself, so maybe I don't want to go there after all.

Smith went to Disneyland last year and he brought back Mickey Mouse ears and they looked really dorky on him. Last year we had show and tell; this year we don't anymore, which is a relief. I hated show and tell. If I went to Disneyland, I wouldn't bother with the ears. Maybe I'd rather go back to Hawaii, anyway. Hawaii was really a lot of fun, and I learned to surf. Well, I didn't perfect it, but I did get so that I could stand up on the board. Also, it was really pretty. The whole shark situation scares me somewhat, though. The Discovery Channel is full of shows about vicious man-eating sharks that live in Hawaii. Come to think of it, I might not want to surf again. Not that anyone is offering to take me on any trips or anything. And of course, with the new baby coming, it's not likely that we'll be going anywhere right away.

" . . . and so he decided to follow his friend out here, because at the time he thought that Edward was his friend."

"Who's Edward?" I ask, forgetting that I wasn't supposed to be listening.

"Brother XII's name was Edward, Carly," he says. "I just said that. Edward Arthur Wilson."

"Huh," I say. "I know *that*. I read it in the book. I thought you meant someone else. A different Edward. Or something."

"Right," he says.

Jenny gets up and starts clearing the table. Normally I have to help her, but in this case I pretend to be really interested in what he is saying so I don't have to help. She doesn't mind. I think she likes it better when I don't help, because sometimes plates jump out of my hands and break. I don't know why. It just happens.

He continues, "There were already a number of houses built for followers just outside of Nanaimo when my grandfather arrived. He was given one of the houses to live in temporarily. He said everyone worked really hard together, doing work on the farmlands and so on, planting potatoes and what have you. He said he learned a lot from Edward, although everyone called him Brother XII, and he was excited about the colony that was forming and excited about the future because he believed that Brother XII was right, that the world was coming towards a time of chaos and from this chaos a great spiritual leader would rise."

I start to yawn, not that this story isn't fascinating or anything. Okay, it's not that interesting. I mean, blah, blah, blah. It's like school. I start eating my dessert very very slowly, one nibble at a time. It is a kind of cake-thing that is covered with fruit, but is still quite delicious. I stab a tiny bite of strawberry and chew it between my two front teeth only. I decide to eat my entire dessert this way.

"Maybe you can just write this down instead of telling me," I say as politely as I can. "Then I can use it for the project."

"But Carly," he says, "I'm getting to the gold."

"Okay, fine," I say. "I have to get up early tomorrow." I yawn again so that he understands that I'm tired. I mean, I have to make the sacrifice of going to bed early so I'm well rested for practice in the morning.

"Okay," he says. "I get it. You're bored. Fine. I'll tell you only about the gold."

"Great," I say. "Thanks."

"Carly," my mum snaps. "Honestly. I thought I raised you to be more polite than this. Apologize right now."

Huh. How embarrassing! "Sorry," I mumble.

"That's okay," he says. "But it is kind of an interesting story. Brother XII was very afraid of banks and of corruption and that sort of thing, so he turned all the money that his followers gave him into gold coins."

"How?" I ask, kind of interested. This sounds good, like perhaps there was some sort of magic involved, not that I'd believe that kind of stuff, but it would be good for the project.

"At the bank," he says. "You could get gold coins at that time instead of paper money."

"Huh," I say. Boring, I think. I should have known.

"Then he took the gold coins and put them in mason jars that were then filled with wax so the coins didn't rattle around, and then they were put in boxes, and then they were buried."

"Where?" I ask.

"No one knows," he says slowly. "There was lots of speculation and lots of people tried to find it, but no one ever did. It might still be out there some- where, or it might just be a story, although . . . "

"What?" I say. "Although what?"

"Although my grandfather always said that he knew where it was buried, and he'd show me before he died."

"And?" I prompt.

"And," he sighs and pushes his floppy hair out of his eyes. "I guess he forgot, because he never did. So we'll never know if there is gold, or there isn't. They did find jars in a hidden cellar underneath Brother XII's house, but there was just a note attached saying *Ha ha, not here.*"

"The note said that?" I say, surprised.

"Not really," he says. "Something like that. Anyway, my grandfather is dead now, and so are most of the people who followed the Brother, and it turned out that he went a little crazy, or maybe he was a little crazy the whole time, and he left and the cabins were all destroyed."

"I know where the site is," Dad says. "Maybe we can go look at it when we get up to the cabin," he adds, looking at me.

"The project will be done by then," I say. "It won't matter anymore."

He looks kind of mad or sad or something when I say this, so I say quickly, "Not that I'm not interested, of course. Whatever. You can show me. It'll be neat. Great." We have kind of a weird relationship because he is not my real dad, but just my step-dad. Sometimes I think I accidentally hurt his feelings when I forget to pretend he isn't the most interesting guy on the planet. My Real Dad was overall much more interesting than this one, but it's not his fault. I try to be nice to this one because I feel sorry for him that he isn't real; he is only a step. Honestly. It's so complicated.

After dinner, we all say our goodbyes to Mr. Taft, and he says, "I'll bring a box of stuff over for you to look through, Carly. Maybe it will help you with your project."

"Thank you," I say sincerely. I mean, that is pretty nice of him considering I was possibly a bit rude when he told his story. If he has good stuff, maybe there's a map in there for finding the treasure.

I go upstairs and I write down some of what he said, though to tell you the truth I don't remember all of it and I fall asleep thinking about Brother XII and the jars of gold. I don't get the part about the wax in the jars. I mean, I like playing with wax from candles as much as the next person, but I think it would be an awful pain to have to dig all the coins out from a big jar of hardened wax. What's the point of making it so difficult? I think maybe Dad is right, maybe this Brother XII was crazy. Which doesn't say much for Mr. Taft's grandfather, does it? Great. Mr. Taft is probably crazy, and he is good friends with my New Dad, so my New Dad is probably crazy also, and the baby will probably be crazy. Super. I sigh and close my eyes and try to think

about diving off that platform without fainting or
falling off until finally I fall asleep.

chapter 3

"Carly, what are you doing up there?" Jon calls through his bullhorn. He uses the bullhorn to talk to us when we are up on the tower because it's hard to hear him when he just shouts.

What I'm doing, to tell you the truth, is just *nothing*. I'm sitting at the end of the platform with my legs dangling off the edge, looking down. Last night, I watched my tape of the Olympics and people did these dives from the platform where they did a handstand first, *but facing the opposite way,* and then used their fingers like little springs and pushed off. When I climbed up here today, I have to admit that I kind of felt like I should try it and so when no one was paying attention, I did a handstand in the middle of the board. I can't believe I did that. As soon as I landed on my feet, I got super dizzy. I mean, really, really dizzy, like I couldn't tell which way was up. Now I'm just sitting here. I can't move. I am completely freaked out, if you know what I mean. Every part of me is shaking. I am going to sit here forever. There is no way I am diving off this thing. Or jumping. Or anything.

"Um, I'm just . . . " I yell. "Just . . . " I can't think of a thing to say. This is horrible. People are starting to notice. I look at my feet and then a million miles below them is the water. I would give all the gold in the world to be in the water right now and not on this board. It's possible that I might cry.

"I'm just thinking for a minute," I call down.

"I'm coming up," he says.

"No!" I say. "Don't!" This is so embarrassing. This makes the whole compass-bleeding-fainting thing seem like awfully small potatoes. This is going to ruin my life. How can I be an Olympic diver if I'm afraid of heights? Not possible. This happened to some kid when we did platform dives for the first time, and he had to quit, he was so embarrassed. I don't want to quit! I love diving.

Maybe I have an ear infection! I remember once a girl at the Olympics had something called verdigris or lumbago or something which was something to do with her ear that caused her to be dizzy. Obviously, that's what I have. Duh! Why didn't I think of that before? I can hear footsteps on the stairs behind me, and I figure it's Jon, so I kind of turn around a bit, but not a lot because for some reason I am afraid to move. It's not Jon. Oh, no no no no no nooo . . .

It's Tim the Nose Blower.

"Hey," he says. "Wazzup?"

"Nothing." I shrug. I'm trying to act casual. Really, this is a very stupid situation. "I think I might have lumbago, that's all."

"Lumbago!" he says. "What's that?"

"I dunno," I say. "Something about your ear that makes you dizzy."

"It is high up," he says.

Is he trying to be nice? What is he doing? He kind of flops down beside me on his belly and hangs his head off the edge. Every part of me wants to scream.

"Would it bug you if I dove?" he says. "I mean, it is my turn and practice is almost over."

"No," I say. Meaning YES.

"Okay, you go first," he says. "But hurry up, I don't have all day."

"Um," I say. "I don't know."

"You've done it a hundred times," he points out. "You can do it one more time. Or I guess you could climb down. You know, if you're scared . . . "

Scared! Huh! Well, I am scared, but I'm not

going to admit it to Tim the Nose Blower. For a second there I forgot that I hate him. I forgot about the nose-blowing incident. I'm a better diver than him! Who is he to "help" me? Where is Jon? Where is Sam? She's supposed to be my friend. I can't see her anywhere. She must be doing some gym work or something. I can see Jon at the side of the pool, looking up at me and sort of shielding his eyes from the sunrise that is streaming in the skylights. I look up at the sky for a second. It's going to be a really beautiful day considering it is still February and not that long ago it snowed. Today it is all clear and the sunrise is very pretty and pink and orange. I like pink and orange together. Maybe I will put some pink and orange in my new room, if I ever get it. If the baby is ever born and Jenny ever moves out.

The carpet in the room has been installed now, and I got to choose it even though it is Jenny's room, which is good. I chose a dark brownish colour. It doesn't sound nice, but it will look really good with pale purple walls. I get kind of lost in thought about my room for a minute, and then I hear the whistle. Jon uses the whistle to get our attention. In this case, now everyone is paying attention to me. Great. Jon kind of gestures at me, like, as if to say, "Do you need help?" And I don't,

I really don't. I just need a minute, or an hour, or a week. No, I'm going to do it. I say to Tim the Nose Blower, "If you don't mind, could you step back a minute, I have to do my dive now." And he does, and I stand up and my legs are only shaking a bit. Well, a good bit, I guess, and I close my eyes and go. It takes like an hour to get to the water, but I do it. I just about cry. Okay, I do cry a little bit in the water, but no one can tell. And then I climb out and Jon says, "Carly, come into my office for a minute." And I think, uh-oh, here we go.

We go in there and I'm shivering a bit because I'm cold. I mean, please. I just got out of the pool. It's February! Think about it. I look at his wall of medals and trophies and the stuff that the Dolphin Diving Club has won and newspaper stories. It is quite interesting. I have a bunch of ribbons and a medal at home. I won two medals last year, but I gave one to my friend Montana as a prize for walking again. She was in a wheelchair for a bit after the accident.

"Well," he says. "What happened?"

"It's possible that I have lumbago," I explained.

"Really?" he says, twinkling his eyes at me. "Why's that?"

"Okay," I say. "I'll tell you the truth. Just between us."

"Just between us," he promises.

"I got dizzy," I say. "I think it's an ear infection."

"Uh huh," he says. "I guess it's possible that you have vertigo."

Vertigo! That's it. Not lumbago. Duh. I wonder what lumbago is. Something stupid, no doubt. No wonder he almost laughed at me.

"It's also possible that you're afraid of heights," he says.

"I'm not," I say firmly.

"No?" he says. "I'll tell you a story, Carly, about when I learned to dive from the platform."

Blah, blah, blah, I think.

"Blah, blah, blah," he says. No he doesn't. I pretend not to pay attention, but really I am listening. Jon is very handsome and smart. He is also a very good diver. Anyway, apparently when he was learning to dive, he was fooling around on the platform with his buddy and his buddy pushed him and he fell and didn't think he was going to hit the water, and after that he freaked out and couldn't do the platform dive for months afterwards. Then he says, "I think maybe if you take a break from the tower, you'll be fine in a little while."

Take a break! No way! So I say, "I don't think so, Jon. I'm sorry you are afraid of heights and whatever, but I'm not." And I march out of his office as stompily as I can. It's hard to stomp with bare feet, but my feet *slap, slap, slap* against the tile. It's a resounding slapping noise. I go straight up the ladder-stairs, which is no small distance. It's ten metres. If you don't know how far that is, I'll tell you. It's far. I mean, you have to climb and turn and climb and turn and climb and turn. It takes most of the stomp out of my step. I'm winded when I get to the top. But when I finally do, I run to the end of the platform and dive like crazy about ten times before I realize that practice is over and everyone else has gone to get ready for school and it's just me and Jon left.

"I think you proved your point, Carly," he says. I can't tell if he's mad or not. Probably, he's just embarrassed because I know he was too scared to do this when he was a kid. I'm not scared of anything. I'm not. Okay, I'm afraid of sharks and ghosts and that sister-thing from my dream the other night, but that's all.

I'm late, so I don't have time to shower properly. All day long I can smell the chlorine in my hair, which is kind of nice. In class, I spend a lot of time sneaking sniffs of my braid and imagining what it will be like to win a gold medal at the Olympics. I sure won't need to know this stuff. I mean, really, who cares which order the planets go in? It's hardly important when you are a world-famous athlete. I listen anyway, sort of. Well, not really. I should pay more attention in school. Sometimes we have surprise quizzes. Ha! Anything with the word "surprise" in front of it should be something good, not something horrendously awful such as a test. I'm trying to focus on listening when someone taps me on the back and passes me a note. It says, *Scaredy-cat!*

"What?" I say out loud. And, of course, then Mrs. Witless says, "Miss Abbott-Fitzgerald? Something you would like to share with the class?"

"No," I say. "I just thought I heard something. I thought I heard the fire alarm!"

The class giggles, and I grin because I like to make everyone laugh, but then she goes over to the corner and writes my name on the detention list right underneath Smith's. Ugh. Detention is bad, but worse when it is with someone you don't know or like. Normally, I get detention with Felicia or Montana for talking in class or what have you, and in that case detention can be quite fun. I turn around and glare at Tim the Nose Blower and he winks.

He *winks.*

Honestly. What a loser. It's too bad he is somewhat cute. I can't believe he would write such a mean note! I thought he was being nice-ish this morning. Well. It just goes to show, like my mum would say. People can let you down. Probably, he was just trying to get me out of the way so he could do his big old show-off dive.

I walk home. It's almost getting dark because it still gets dark pretty early, particularly when you have detention. Detention wasn't so bad, as it turned out. Mrs. Witless let Smith and I play chess because it is an educational game, and she had a headache. The only rule was that we couldn't talk. It is quite hard to play chess without talking. For example, at the "Checkmate!" part we had to gesture wildly. Smith is funnier than I thought he would be. He isn't even that weird-looking when you look at him closely and you see where his hair ends and his skin begins. Not that we are friends or anything. Not a bit.

After dinner, Mum comes up to my room and says, "Carly, you should have a bath, you stink like chlorine." Um, nice. Thanks. "Fine," I say. "I wouldn't want to *stink*."

"Don't get mad," she says. "You are very quick to get mad these days."

Am I? I don't know if that is true. Of course, I have a lot to deal with, what with the platform diving. Not to mention gymnastics twice a week. I don't even know if I like gymnastics anymore. I kind of want to just do diving. But gymnastics is fun. There are benefits. For example, it is good exercise, and it makes my muscles strong, which is important for diving. I don't go to many meets and stuff, though, because they are usually at the same time as diving meets. Huh. My life is very hectic.

"I might be less stressed if I had a new room," I tell her, meanly.

"We've been through that," she says. "I don't want to do that again."

"Fine," I say. "What do you want? I have to take a bath."

"I'll run it for you," she says. Which is nice, because she runs the best baths. She puts stuff in it, like flower buds and junk involving little leaves and petals. They smell nice, although they stick to you when you get out and you have to kind of scrape them off with the towel.

I climb into the tub and she offers to wash my hair, so I let her. If you have never had anyone else wash your hair, I'm telling you, you should try it. It is like a tiny massage on your head. Then she dumps the rinse water on and it all runs into my eyes.

"OUCH!" I scream. "What did you do that for?"

"I didn't mean to," she says. "Calm down. You aren't six years old."

Meanwhile, my eyes are stinging like someone has thrown acid in them and I'm clawing at the towel to try to get the sting out.

"Get out!" I yell. "I don't need that kind of help!"

"Don't yell at me!" she yells back. "I'm your mother!"

"But you're yelling at me!" I yell.

She gets up and glares at me and turns and leaves the room. Well. Now I'm all upset. I sink down in the tub and keep only my eyes and nose above the level of the water. I stick my toes up onto the cool ceramic tile. I should paint my toenails, I think. There is a tiny bit of nail polish on them but it is mostly chipped off. I am thinking about that when there is a little knock on the door.

"Carly?"

"Um, yes?"

"It's me, Jenny. Can I come in?"

"Sure," I tell her. Why not? Everyone else just wanders in when I'm in the tub and pours shampoo in my eyes; she might as well, too. She sits down on the toilet. Well, not *on* the toilet. It's closed. You know what I mean.

"I thought I heard some . . . "

"Yelling?" I fill in for her.

"Yes," she says. "Is everything okay?"

"Mum's just so . . . " I shrug. "I don't know. I'm tired of her being pregnant and in a bad mood and mad."

"I can understand that," says Jenny. "But have you ever been pregnant?"

"Me?" I say, outraged. "I'm ten years old! What are you talking about?"

"Well," she says. "I was just thinking that I've never been pregnant, and I don't know much about what it's like. And you've never been pregnant, so you don't know what it's like. So, maybe it's harder than we think; maybe it makes your mum more tired than usual and more sensitive and just more irritable, and maybe we should cut her some slack."

"I guess," I mumble, blowing bubbles in the water.

"Okay, then," she says, and she gets up and leaves.

What was *that* all about? I think. It's a good thing Jenny is so nice. She can get away with giving me almost-lectures without me getting mad. I turn the tap on and add more hot water until it is so hot I can hardly stand it. There is steam rising up all around me. It's like being in a witch's stew.

Knock-knock.

"What *now?*" I say.

"Carly, it's me," says Mum. "Can I come back in?"

"Whatever," I say. She comes in and sits right down on the edge of the bath, even though it's all wet.

"Sorry," I tell her, staring off into the distance.

"That's okay," she says. "I'm sorry, too."

She swirls the water around me, and we sit and stare at each other for a minute. Her eyes are pink like she's been crying, which makes me feel bad again.

"How about you help me think of some names for the baby?" she says suddenly.

"Really?" I say. "Can I?" I mean, I have lots of opinions on the whole name situation, but she never asked me before. "Okay," I tell her. "I'll make a list." I'm good at making lists. It is one of my skills. Also, I am very good at knowing what is a good name and what isn't. For example, the baby's name can't be "Zane" because that would rhyme with "Shane" which would be stupid. The entire Marly/Carly situation is bad enough. I start thinking about the name right away. It has to be something that sounds good with Fitzgerald, but also with Carly, Marly and Shane. Carly, Marly, Shane and _____ . Hmmmm. *Harley*. I giggle and lie back in the hot soapy water and Mum pours hot water over my hair to rinse the conditioner out of it, this time keeping her hands over my eyes so nothing goes in there. This is super nice. It is a real treat. Normally, I just shower at the pool.

"It might help you if you see the baby first," she says.

"*See* it?" I say. That's silly, I think. I don't want to wait until July to start thinking up names. I mean, really. Besides, deciding on a name takes time, and you can't wait until it's born and then just leave it nameless until you figure something out. Then it would be called "Baby" forever, which would be horrendous. Or maybe just "Fitzgerald." I wonder if that is why Smith is named Smith. Maybe his parents couldn't be bothered to give him a first name and just let him use his last name for everything. That's quite sad, really, if you think about it. Poor Smith.

"Yes," Mum says. "See it. I was thinking if there isn't anything too important going on at school tomorrow, you could come with me to see the baby."

"Huh?" I say. "What? How?" Then I add, "School

is never important," and roll my eyes. "Please."

As it turns out, she is going to have some test tomorrow where they take some kind of X-ray picture of the baby and look at it and measure its head and legs and arms and so on and so forth. It's only four months old, so I didn't think it would look much like a baby yet, but I guess it does. Who knew? I wonder how big it is. This is quite exciting. I don't know how I'll be able to sleep, I'm so agog. I love the word *agog*. It was our word of the day in Language Arts yesterday. I'm trying to use it at least once every day now.

"Will we be able to see if it's a boy or a girl?" I ask as she tucks me into bed. My hair smells great. She blew it dry for me and everything.

"I don't know," she says. "Would you want to know? You don't want it to be a surprise?"

Hmmmm. I don't know if I do or not. I fall asleep thinking about names. I think I like the name Zoe for a girl. Zoe is a good name. It goes nicely with Fitzgerald because of the *Z*.

The hospital is the same as I remember from visiting Montana. It stinks and there are people in the hallways. Honestly. It's nuts. Why do they have to sleep in the hall? You would think that putting them in a room — even a crowded room —

would be better than leaving them out here. They must be quite embarrassed to be lying there sleeping when people walk by. Think about it. I would not enjoy lying in the hallway myself. Although you might meet some interesting people that come to visit other people. That would be okay. Shane, who is a bit of a baby — after all, he is not even three — starts to cry when we walk past this really old man who is sound asleep with his mouth open. You could drop stuff in there. He looks like the same old man who was lying there last time I was here. That is quite tragic, I think. Also I think it is rude that Shane cried; it's not the old man's fault that he is a bit frightening to look at. None of the people in the hall are awake, come to think of it, and they are all mostly very old, except for this one lady who looks quite young-ish. I stare at her for a minute before my mum pulls me away.

We go down one hall and then another and I think we are probably quite lost. This hospital is like a secret world with a hundred different secret tunnels and so on. It is a bit scary, or it would be if I were by myself. We walk and walk and walk for what feels like six hours before we finally find the right desk, and Mum checks in. And me and Dad and Marly and Shane go sit down on the seats to wait. This is a whole family kind of adventure, as you can tell. While we wait, I read a magazine article about lipstick. There are different ways of applying lipstick. Did you know this? There is also a trick where you stick your finger in your mouth and pull it out to avoid getting lipstick on your teeth. I make a mental note to remember this if, in fact, I am ever old enough to wear lipstick. Next weekend I will turn eleven. Eleven! I am almost a teenager, and I feel sure that lipstick is allowed on teenagers by law. I spend some time thinking about getting my ears pierced. I'm definitely going to do it, I decide. It will probably only hurt for a second. If it hurt every time you put earrings in or took them out, then no one would do it.

Eventually, after we wait forever and Marly is whining and complaining because she is hungry, and Shane has had to use the bathroom about ten times, we are allowed in to see Mum. She is lying on a table and has clear, shiny goo all over her balloon belly. It looks like hair gel. Montana uses gel in her hair now that it is short. Using gel in long hair is a mistake, as I'm sure you know, because it makes your hair a bit crunchy, which is not very pretty on long hair. Also, it makes your hair next to impossible to brush. My hair is quite long now, as I am growing it out. It is past my shoulders and near my elbows when I lean forward. Gel is good on short hair; it makes it more fun and pixie-ish. Anyway, I don't think this stuff is hair gel; it is some kind of hospital gel or whatever that makes it so we can see the baby. The lady who is doing the test is very stern-looking, not unlike Mrs. Witless. She takes this wand-thing and presses it quite hard on Mum's belly. I know it is quite hard because her belly kind of dents in a bit where it is being poked.

"I have to pee!" Mum whispers to me, which makes me laugh. She is pretty funny sometimes. I mean, there is a time and a place to pee and this clearly would be a very bad time.

After a couple of minutes of this the lady says, "Look! Look!" She is all excited, and we look at the screen thing — it's like a TV, sort of, but black and white — and there it is! There is a weird-looking big-headed baby-thing! My little brother or sister or whatever! It is super exciting in a creepy sort of way. Being able to look inside my mum's belly is a little strange. If she had eaten a big sandwich for breakfast, would we have seen it? I wonder. I also wonder what else they can see with that thing. Can they see your brain? Your heart? What? It's neat, and I try to remember everything so I can tell Montana. She will need to know about stuff like this if she is going to be a doctor, after all.

Then Shane says, "Look at that baby! Holy cow!" It's really cute, so we all laugh. He is cute sometimes. Maybe I wish he was around all the time like this, and not just on weekends. No. I only wish that when he is being cute, not when he is being a brat, which is approximately nine-tenths of the time as far as I can tell.

Marly says, "Is it a girl baby?"

The technician smiles at her and says, "Don't you want it to be a surprise?"

And Marly says, "No. I wanna know." I'm glad she said it and not me, because I want to know, too, but I didn't want to ask. The technician looks at my mum and my mum shakes her head and says, "Sorry kids, I want it to be a surprise, I think."

"Darn," I say. "It's much easier to think of names when you know if it's going to be a girl or a boy. Duh."

"Let's think of names for both," she says, "And then it won't matter."

Then my dad kind of holds her hand and they stare at each other all mushily and they gaze at the screen and say, "Our baby, our baby." Oh brother, I think. Here we go.

I only hope they don't love this baby the best. I

mean, it's their baby, as opposed to me (I'm just Mum's) and the others (they're just Dad's). I wish my Real Dad didn't have to die, I think suddenly. I get kind of teary, to tell you the truth. I mean, if he didn't die, I wouldn't have to worry about all this, would I? This puts me in kind of a bad mood, and on the way home in the car I kick Marly. This results in there being Big Trouble and, instead of getting to go out for a nice lunch, we end up eating tofu sandwiches at home and then I have to walk to school for afternoon classes.

Huh. This special day kind of got wrecked, don't you think? And worse than that, there is a surprise quiz in Science and I get a terrible mark because I wasn't paying attention when we learned about the planets. For goodness' sake!

After the quiz, I start making lists of names to give to Mum and Dad at dinner so they won't stay mad at me. So far, I have: Zoe, Grace and Madeleine for a girl; and Zachary, Noel and Zeke for a boy. I like the Z names a lot right now. I wish my name started with a Z, although Zarly would be a very, very bad name.

It's Wednesday again, so after school I walk over to Marly's daycare and pick her up for piano, and we hop onto the bus and go downtown for her lesson. Downtown is very exciting and interesting. There are lots of stores and also a McDonald's. One day, I might be brave enough to go to McDonald's while Marly is at her lesson, but today I stay and listen to her class bang away on the piano and the xylophone and the little metal triangles. It is very noisy. I don't like Marly much, but I must say she is much better at the piano than all these other brats. I am sort of proud of her. I wonder what our new sister/brother will be good at. I mean, I'm good at diving, and Marly is good at piano, and Shane isn't good at anything yet because he is too little, but he can read, so he is obviously very smart. I hope that our new brother/sister is smart.

On the bus on the way home, we talk about names and stuff. Marly likes the name "Felicity," but this is only because her best friend is named Felicity. She isn't very good at thinking up names, let me tell you. Felicity is about the only name she can come up with other than Mike, who is also a boy at her daycare. Not very original. I do think it's a bit neat that we are talking about our new sister/brother, though it makes me think that maybe when Marly grows up a bit we will be friends and when we are mums, maybe our kids will play together and so on. The rest of the ride we spend blowing on the windows and drawing happy faces, and that takes care of that.

Oh, I almost forgot. There is one more big surprise today that I didn't expect. And that is that Dad is going to take me and Montana and Felicia and Mr. Taft up to the cabin this weekend and we are going to explore Brother XII's old site and take pictures and stuff for our project! I could not believe it when he told me. I was like, "What? Are you crazy? It's February!" And he said, "It's your birthday surprise! And this weekend it will be March, remember?" And I went, "Goodness, you're right!" Wheeee! This will be the best birthday ever. I have never been to the cabin when it wasn't summer. I can't wait. It's even worth missing diving practice for.

I should tell you that the cabin is my favourite place in the world, except for maybe Hawaii. Although at the cabin there is no risk of being eaten by sharks, which is a plus in its favour. I love going to the cabin with friends more than anything — and without Marly and Shane! Wow. This is going to be a perfect weekend, a perfect adventure. It is going to make this stupid, boring project worthwhile.

Right away I call Montana and she says, "Did

your dad tell you?" And I say, "Yup!" And we both start talking at once. We have to try to find some kind of clue as to where to look for the gold, so tomorrow after school I am going to dig through Mr. Taft's grandfather's stuff which is in a box in the Other Room.

"This is like Nancy Drew!" Montana says.

"Totally," I agree, although I secretly think this is going to be much, much better than that. I mean, Nancy Drew never found millions of dollars in gold coins. I say, "We'll have to invite Sam. What about the Gold Diggers Club?"

We had forgotten about her, sort of. I guess because Sam doesn't go to our school we didn't think of her. She was with us though, when we made up the Gold Diggers Club at the end of last summer. Right away, I hang up and run and ask Dad, and he says, "Sure, you can invite her. There's room because Mum isn't coming, and the other kids are too little." So I call her up, and her mum talks to my mum and, finally, it's all settled. The Gold Diggers Club is back in action!

chapter 4

When we get up on Saturday, it's still dark. It isn't any earlier than I usually get up for diving, but it seems earlier because I still have to do a bunch of stuff to get ready. For example, I have to put on layers of clothing because Dad says it will be cold on the boat, and I have to open one birthday present, which Mum says I can open before we go, even though I have to wait for the rest of my presents until Sunday night when we come home. I hurry through the getting dressed part, and put on lots of things such as several pairs of leggings and sweatpants. I can hardly bend my legs, there is so much clothing going on. By the time I get to the kitchen, Mum and Dad are both up but look really sleepy and annoyed for being awake so early. Mum is making me pancakes, which are my favourite, because it's my birthday. It's my birthday, yippeee! I love birthdays. They are the best. The present is on the table and it is quite big and wrapped up with very nice paper that has things on it like starfish and so on. I didn't ask for anything specific, so I don't know what this could be. Normally, I ask for something; like last year I really wanted a bike, and the year before that I really, really wanted a puppy. This year, I had no clue what to ask for. Stupid, huh? I couldn't think of anything. So to tell you the truth, I'm a tiny bit nervous about opening this because I honestly have no idea what it is. It could be anything. What if it is something that I hate? What will I say?

I eat my pancakes first, and they are especially delicious because they have chocolate chips in them and M&M's. They are like very small individual cakes. The kids are still asleep, so it is just me and Mum and Dad, which is also nice. I get the feeling that after the baby is born, this won't happen much. Well, ever. This may be the last time! They are both yawning like mad, though, and Dad keeps looking at his watch because we have to get out to the boat and get to a certain point in the trip before a specific time. This place is called Porlier Pass and we have to get there when the tide is at a certain point, otherwise the current is too strong. Dad really sweats a great deal about this Porlier Pass, so I know all about it. Trust me. He even taught me to read the tide tables, so I know what he means. We have to get there by 9:30 a.m. Or else. Porlier Pass is where the biggest octopuses in the world live. I would hate to sink in Porlier Pass and have to swim through all the tentacles. That would be disgusting. Although I read once that if you are attacked by an octopus you should bite the little knob on its head very hard and it will let you go. I'm not sure I'm up for this, frankly. Best to avoid it by being on time, I think.

"Hurry up and open your gift!" Dad says, looking at his watch.

"Okay, okay," I say, and I tear into the paper. I don't know what it is. What is it? It's a *thing.* "What is it?" I ask. "What?"

"It's a metal detector," Mum says. As soon as she says that, right away I can tell. A metal detector! So we can find the gold! We already have a map in my backpack that shows where the cabins were. It isn't exactly a treasure map, but close enough.

"Hurray!" I say. "Thank you so much! Thank you!" I go and hug her and grab the metal detector. Dad is pretty much pushing me out the door. I barely have time to grab my backpack. Mr. Taft is waiting by the car in the dark. He kind of scared me. I didn't see him there. We have to hurry and pick up Montana and Felicia and Sam, and then we're on our way!

Lucky for us, the water is super calm. It's kind of spooky bombing along in the boat in the dim light of early morning. There are no other boats around for some reason. I don't know why not. It is certainly very, very cold out here on the water, but it will warm up later, I'm sure. Although there are some dark and somewhat ugly clouds up ahead. Dad and Mr. Taft sit up on the top part of the boat, which is called the "flying bridge." I don't know why it is called this. A "flying bridge" sounds like something that would involve a bridge, for one thing, and this is just two little seats on the top of the boat without a roof so that you can see better.

Montana and Felicia and Sam and me sit downstairs. It's funny not having a dog or two around, but Mum wanted the dogs at home to look after her. I don't know what the dogs could possibly do to help her in an emergency, but I know how she feels. Roo and Blue both love the cabin, and I'm sure they knew we were going because they recognized my backpack and stuff. I could hear them yowling when we drove down the street. I think they were very upset to be left out. She could have at least let us take one of them. What if we need protection?

Never mind that. I'm sure they'll be fine. They don't like the boat that much to begin with.

"Let's see what you have!" Montana says. She is super excited and has a camera and everything to take pictures of the site. Honestly, she is very keen about school.

"Do you think that metal thing will work?" Sam asks. She is more interested in the gold, I can tell. Well, of course she is. She doesn't even go to our school, so she doesn't have to worry about this dumb project.

I let Sam open the box and I go into my backpack and pull out the notes I made. I can tell the girls are surprised because normally I'm not that excited about school and so on, but Mr. Taft helped me and in his grandfather's stuff we found some notes and so on which I thought would be helpful. I didn't want to bring his original stuff because it was pretty old and crumbly and so forth, so I wrote it out. I covered the map with plastic so it doesn't get wrecked. Like I said, it doesn't say where the treasure is but it shows where they brought their boat in and the path they took across the island, and the location of

Brother XII's cabin and so on. It is all quite far from my cabin, on a whole other bay. I don't look forward to walking that far, so I hope we take the boat. It looks like about a hundred miles or so, but Dad says it's only five or six. Five or six is too far. Trust me. Besides, it will be hard to walk in all these layers.

By the time we arrive in the bay, it is 10:00 already and the sun is out. The bay is really protected and is made from that sandstone rock, so it is almost too warm in that area for all these layers. I take off my outer two layers of leggings and stuff them in my bag. The girls are all excited and point things out to Felicia, who is the only one who hasn't been here before. Montana points to the middle of the bay and says, "There's the rock that I dove off when I broke my back."

Then there is a big silence as we all stare at the rock and remember what happened. It makes me very sad, to tell you the truth. I would do anything to undo that last dive we did that time, I promise you that.

Dad calls from the rowboat, "What's going on, girls?"

And we yell, "Nothing." And we hurry to cross the little bridge on the wharf and climb around the bay on the rocks. The bags and stuff have to be rowed across because the rocks are kind of steep when the tide is up this high. There are a lot of dangerous places where you might fall in the water. I am a little worried about Montana, but she swings around on the rocks like a gymnast, which she used to be until the accident. There is no need for me to worry, I remind myself. Sometimes I worry too much, and then I worry about worrying too much. You can see how this gets out of hand quickly.

We walk through the woods to the cabin, which is interesting because it really looks nothing like it does in the summer. For one thing, there is hardly any stinging nettle and so on. I guess it dies off in the winter. The moss isn't as green and all the grasses and so forth are just starting to peek through the soil. It is all familiar, and yet unfamiliar at the same time. We trudge along for a while with Dad and Mr. Taft yacking away. Mr. Taft thinks everything is "fantastic!" He is really excited to be here where his grandfather lived for a while. I don't have a grandfather, but I guess if I did I might be interested in where he lived. Maybe.

I notice that Montana is kind of lagging behind a bit, so I wait for her and we walk together. She gets very sad when she gets tired, like she's frustrated that she can't keep up. I can't say that I blame her. She used to be very energetic and so on. It hasn't even been a year, though, since the accident, so I guess it is to be expected. I wait for Sam and Felicia to notice that we're lagging behind, and they do and they run back. They are both talking at once. Felicia has never been anywhere where there are no cars or roads or electricity. She can hardly believe such a place exists.

"It's so quiet!" she keeps saying.

We pass this tree that I love to climb, so we stop for a few minutes and climb the tree. I stay on the low branches with Montana because the weirdest thing happens when I'm climbing and that is I suddenly get nervous and dizzy-ish. I can't believe it. I refuse to be afraid of heights. Why is this happening? I force myself to look up at Felicia and Sam, but it makes me dizzy. Seriously. Well, I don't want to make a big deal of it now. We have a lot to do. Sam goes right up to the top and dangles from her arms.

"Don't fall," I say crossly. "Don't fool around. It's stupid."

"Girls!" Dad calls. "Hurry up! We have to get to the cabin and get ready to head up to the site if we want to fit everything in today!"

Phew. We scamper down the tree and run to

catch up. I whisper to Dad, when I get a chance, that I think we should take the boat because I don't think Montana can walk that far. He looks surprised, but then he remembers and says, "That's a great idea, Carly. We'll take the little run-about with the engine on it! I think we'll all fit."

The cabin is all sealed up for winter. Before we leave at the end of the summer, Dad puts plastic over all the windows. One time he didn't do it, and we got to the cabin for the first trip of the year and the windows were shattered. I guess some people had come up to the island to go hunting because there are lots of deer here and so on. I don't think it should be allowed, but I'm just a kid so I can hardly stop it. They are allowed to hunt from October to March or something like that. Dad figures that some idiots were fooling around and shooting at things from the beach and shot out our windows. I'm not kidding. We found bullets buried in the back wall. It was super scary, and now he puts boards over the windows as well as plastic. Not that that would stop a bullet, but he says it "minimizes the temptation." It must work, because it hasn't happened since, although the cabin has been broken into a bunch of times. I'm kind of nervous when we round the last bend and the roof comes into sight, because what if there is a burglar in there right now? What if a hunter is in there and he has a gun? You never know, these things can happen.

I guess I look kind of scared because Sam whispers, "What's wrong?" And I shake my head and say brightly, "Oh, nothing!" I mean, she's a guest. I don't want her to be nervous.

Dad goes and unlocks the doors and starts to take down the wood and we all rush into the cabin and there is no one there. Of course. Which is a great relief, but at the same time I feel let down. It is just the same, only it has the musty, locked-up, damp smell it gets when it isn't being used. We all climb up into the loft and choose our beds for the night and unpack our backpacks. Felicia and Sam are going to use the bunk beds and me and Montana are going to use the camp cots. The loft is fun to sleep in because you can only get to it on a ladder. The sleeping bags are pretty musty and stinky, so Dad says we can hang them outside while we get the boat ready for our adventure.

Putt-putt-putt. The little engine has to work super hard to carry the weight of all of us plus our lunch basket and our cameras and our metal detector. The water is not so calm anymore; it is getting a small bit windy, which isn't good for such a tiny boat. Once, when Dad and the kids were out here on the boat, there was a big pod of killer whales, which was quite exciting and also nerve-wracking. We are keeping our eyes open for whales and at the same time we are huddling together because it might be sunny right now but it is quite cold-ish.

Finally we get to what we think is the right place and we pull the boat up on the shore. On the beaches around our cabin, the shore is quite steeply sloped sandstone, but here it is very flat, like poured concrete. It is quite interesting how different it is even though it's so close. There is also a neat bar of sand that Dad says is a "spit." It connects the flat sandstone beach to a reef-type thing. It is neat, and I wish we had one closer to our cabin. It forms a perfect swimming hole in the sea. Not that we can swim today, it's way too cold.

I follow the others up a steep path and into the woods. There are some cabins right on the beach but no one is in them and they are new cabins, not Brother XII cabins. Besides, I read in the notes that the cabins were built well back from the water because it is warmer when you aren't facing right into the wind. Speaking of which, it is getting a bit windier. I can see Dad looking back at the sea every once in a while with his "concerned" face. He worries a lot about the sea and the wind, though, so it's hard to know when to take it seriously. Up and up we climb, deep into thickets of salal and huge trees. This isn't much of a "site," I can tell you that. The concept of a "site" makes you think of a flattish area with houses, but this is truly just a super-steep hill with no houses. After a while of climbing, Mr. Taft shouts, "Over here!" So we all rush over, and he is standing in the middle of a grassy bit and there are a few logs lying there. Logs! Huh. Big deal. "This is the foundation of a house," he explains. I am quite disappointed, but don't let on. I had it in my head that we would find haunted houses and that type of thing. Obviously, I've been reading too many mystery books. Darn.

"That's IT?" says Sam. "Boring!" I'm glad she said it, because I completely agree. Just then Montana calls, "Over here!" She has found an old broken plate, which is a bit more interesting and closer to being a treasure. It is very dirty, but you can tell that it used to be very nice and expensive. Hmmm. Funny that they lived in cabins but had nice china. I mean, we use plastic dishes at the cabin. I don't know why, come to think of it. It just is a cabin-type thing to do.

We dig around in the bushes with the metal detector, but the only metal thing we find is a rusty old rake and also a bottle cap. It is super difficult to make sense of the map when you are actually in the woods and there are no land-marks. We follow the trail for a bit and look for obvious places, such as caves or weird-looking things. We do find one big rock that looks out of place and we use the metal detector like crazy, but it doesn't beep. It is very exhausting work, let me tell you.

After we've given up, Dad takes pictures of us on the house foundation for our project. I pretend I am not disappointed, although I am quite a bit. Imag-ine the look on everyone's face in the class if we came in with a bunch of jars full of wax and gold! We would get an *A* for sure, and Tim the Nose Blow-er would be crazily jealous and probably he would start to like me because I was rich. Of course, I don't want to be liked for my money. Not that I have any. But if I did. You know what I mean.

We eat our lunch, which is squished sandwich-es, and then we venture back up the path, farther and farther. There are lots of old foundations of houses, which are interesting in spite of the fact they aren't gold. You can almost imagine what it would be like to live here. It is crazily quiet in the woods. You can hardly even hear the sea from here, just the clucking sounds of different birds or squirrels.

I'm getting quite sweaty in my layers from all this walking. "How are you doing?" I ask Montana, but she is snapping pictures of the bush and stuff and says, "Fine!" I don't know why I worry about her. She's so fired up by this project that she is up for anything, I'm sure! I run up ahead. I like to run sometimes. I am very energetic and didn't have diving today, so I have excess energy I suppose. I'm running and running, and then OOOF! I trip! Honestly. How clumsy. The wind is knocked out of me for a quick second, and I gasp for breath, and as I'm lying there on the cold dirt path I look to the left and I see something! It looks like a jar. My heart starts beating really fast and I croak, "Everyone!"

"Carly!" says Mr. Taft. "Goodness! Are you all right?"

I nod and scramble to my feet. "Look!" I whisper. I'm thinking about the jars of wax and gold, of course. He sees what I'm seeing. It's in a little caved-in hole at the bottom of a tree. He reaches in and pulls it out and passes it to me. It's very dirty, but heavy. I can't believe it! I'm grinning like mad.

"Felicia! Montana! Sam!" I call, and they strag-
gle up the path.

"What is it?" they say. Sam is holding the metal
detector and she sees the jar and right away holds
out the detector thing, which beeps like crazy.

"Oh my goodness!" says Montana. "Open it!"

The jar is sealed tight. I pull and pull, but I
can't open the little hinges that keep the lid on. I
give up and pass it to Dad, who pries it open with
his knife. I close my eyes! This could be it! The
gold! But why would it be so easy? It seems . . .

"Carrots!" says Dad, laughing. "Look, Carly!" I
open my eyes and peek. He's right. Those are
some very old, very bad-looking CARROTS. Huh. I
am totally crushed. I mean it. I thought for sure it
was the gold.

Just at that moment, there is a gust of wind
and it is quite strong. Dad jumps up and says,
"Uh-oh!" I can tell that he is worried because he
forgot to fret about the weather for about ten minutes.

He dashes away ahead of us, back down the
path, yelling to Mr. Taft to walk down with us. I'm
kind of mad because I wanted to find the gold, but
at the same time I can understand how he wants
to check the weather. The funny thing about the
cabin is how much the weather means. At home,

a bad day is just a bad, boring day. But here, a bad weather day can be a big old disaster. We get down to the beach finally, and Dad has pulled the boat up really high. He looks at Mr. Taft and kind of raises his eyebrows and then he says, "Looks like we'll have to sit this one out."

I look across the Georgia Strait, which is what the water is called here, towards Vancouver, which is a hundred hours or so away. There is the strangest line of huge black clouds galloping across the sky towards us. Under the clouds, the waves are churning up. It is way, way too rough to take the boat back to the cabin. My heart does a little *lub-dub* of fear, to tell you the honest to Pete truth. How did this happen? It was such a nice day! Also, it's my birthday! Disasters are not supposed to happen on a person's birthday. It's against all the rules.

I shiver a bit and notice the other girls look a bit scared, so I say, "I'm sure it'll pass really soon." I don't feel very sure of that, though, because just then it gets quite dark and the clouds are right overhead.

"I guess this is why we don't come to the cabin in the winter very often," Dad mutters.

"It's March," I argue.

"Yes," he says, "but it's still winter!"

I guess that's true. I didn't think of it that way.

"We're going to need some shelter," Mr. Taft says, squinting up at the sky. He's right, because you won't believe what happens next! I'll tell you, but you still won't believe it.

The dark clouds open up . . .

And it starts to *snow*. But not pretty, soft snow like we had a few weeks ago at home. This is a different thing altogether. It is windy, cold and blowing hard little pellets of snow.

Oh my goodness.

What are we going to do?

chapter 5

The waves are crashing up over the rocks and we are huddled together shivering. Dad and Mr. Taft have gone to look for some shelter, and in the meantime, we are in a little dip behind an old rotten log, protected a bit by the shrubs and stuff. It is freezing. I can't believe this is happening! It's outrageous. None of us says very much because I think we are all stunned and also our teeth are chattering.

Then Montana says, "No one is going to believe this!"

And Felicia says, "Imagine if this happened in the winter when Brother XII was here. He wouldn't have been burying gold, that's for sure. He'd be inside by the fire."

We all agree. Where would he bury it? The other thing I think of right away is that there aren't many places to bury things here as the island is mostly sandstone, which, as I'm sure you know, is impossible to dig. It's rock, for goodness' sake. I kind of start wondering if maybe he didn't put it somewhere else, like maybe he hid it on a different island. There are lots of islands around here that you could get to very easily if it wasn't super stormy. Or maybe he didn't bury it, maybe he hid it in a cave. There are some sandstone caves and so forth that were created by the wind and the sea smashing away at the beach over millions of years. Also, there are lots of rocks that have fallen down on the beach and maybe there are caves behind them. This is worth exploring, but obviously not now. Not in a majorly catastrophic snowstorm. I can't believe how hard I'm shivering. The other girls are all bright red in the face and shaking, too. It is possible that we will all get pneumonia and die. Think about it. We can't get back to our cabin — it is way too far to walk and we have nowhere to go.

"Girls!" Dad calls.

"Yes?" we all yell at the same time. It is hard to hear him because of the way the wind is howling like Roo howls when she hears an ambulance siren or something. He comes up to us; his cheeks are bright red and he has snow stuck in his hair. I shriek at first because I thought he was really far away and it turns out he is right here.

"We're going to have to get into one of these cabins," he says.

"Break in?" I say. "We can't do that!" I mean, I know what it's like to arrive at your cabin and find out that someone else has been in it. It's very unpleasant, I can tell you that.

"We have to," he says. The snow is really swirling around him now, and the noise that the waves make is like thunder. "I'd understand if someone broke into our cabin in the same situation, wouldn't you?"

"Not really," I mumble, but I follow him because I really don't have much choice. The cabin that we are going to break into is a little bit back from the beach. It looks nice-ish, but not as nice as ours. Also, it is all boarded up and so on and locked. The only way I can see to get in would be to break a window and then it would be freezing inside as well, and also breaking someone else's window is just plain wrong.

Mr. Taft is waiting for us on the deck of the cabin. "I can't get in," he says to Dad. "It's locked up tight as a drum. Maybe we should try the other one."

"Too far away," Dad says. "We have to get inside!"

We all stare at the building. I'm starting to feel

numb all over, to tell you the truth. The cabin is tall. It is two storeys high. Also, it has a chimney, which means it has a fireplace, which means we can have a fire! I'd do anything to get into that cabin, I can tell you that right now. I jump up and down a bit to keep warm. Out of the corner of my eye I notice that Sam is crying a little bit, but pretending not to. Sam! And she is so brave. I act like I don't notice, but I know I have to get my friends inside right away. I shuffle over to Dad and say quietly, "Dad, what about up there?" I point up at the top floor of the cabin where there is a window that is not boarded up. I can't tell from here if it's locked or not, but there's even a really tall wooden ladder leading up to it.

"The ladder won't hold me," he says. "It's rotten. I think we're going to have to break some glass." I look up at the window, which looks about a million miles away through the falling snow. The snow is starting to stick to our shoes and the ground and stuff. If I wasn't so cold, I might think it was all kind of neat. From inside, this would be very exciting!

"I'll do it," I say.

"What?" he says. "No way, Carly, it isn't safe."

"But, Dad," I say, "if we break this window, all the cold air will come in."

"We'll board it up," he says. "Let's do it. Gary!" he calls.

"Dad . . . " I say, and I grab the ladder and scramble up it. I can feel the rungs breaking under my feet and halfway up I get that "Uh-oh, this is a bad idea!" feeling, and at the top I try to pry up the window and it doesn't open and I look down and get that horrible dizzy feeling which is made worse by the snow. What am I doing? I must have lost my mind! I'm scared of heights, remember? Well, I remind myself, it's not like you have to jump off the ladder or anything. Besides, it's not *that* far.

The window is square and small. There is no way Dad would have fit through it even if the ladder wasn't rotten. I have to get in, because if I don't, and if I fall off this ladder, I will be totally in trouble for disobeying and putting myself in danger and blah, blah, blah.

I wiggle the window a bit more, trying to put as little weight on the rungs of the ladder as possible. I can feel it sort of creaking and stuff. I glance down really fast and I see Dad holding onto it. He is squinting, but I can't tell if he is mad. I'm sure he is. Ooooh, boy. I gouge away at the sides of the window with my fingers, trying to see which part might be loose. It's taking ages, and I'm getting a little freaked out. Some of the rungs broke on my way up; I don't think I could get down that way.

I am starting to panic, to tell you the truth, and I pull and push at the glass like mad. And then I figure it out! All at once it gives a bit. It opens from top to bottom, not bottom to top or side to side. Duh! Once I work my fingers into the little edge part (without looking down!), it is pretty easy to do, and then I just fall through the window. I'm sure everyone is yelling at me, but luckily I can't hear them because of the wind.

I land on what feels like concrete, but it turns out that it is a bed. A pretty uncomfortable bed, mind you. It is very, very dark in here and it takes a few minutes for my eyes to adjust to the shadows. I stumble around a bit, hoping I don't fall down the hole to the lower floor. All the cabins here have no stairs, just holes with ladders leading to the other level. Finally I find it, after I bonk my head about ten times on the beams, and I climb down, breaking cobwebs with my feet. I hate cobwebs. They completely gross me out, the way they stick to your skin and you can't get them off. They are worse than the spiders, if you want my opinion. I trip over a little table and land on my belly and it takes me a minute to get my breath and then, finally, I get to the door, which I unlock and open.

"Come on in!" I yell, but I guess they don't hear me because they are around the back. I prop the door open just in case it is one of those doors that lock automatically when you close them, and I run around through the blizzard. I don't know if this is an actual blizzard or not, but I imagine this is what a blizzard would be like, although I've never seen one before. Well, I've seen them on TV, but it is hard to tell what they are actually like until you are in one. I don't want to stay out in this one for long, I can tell you that. I can't believe how much warmer it is inside out of the wind.

"Hey!" I yell. "Heeeeyyy!" They all look around and come running, except for Montana, who kind of just walks fast. She is trying to be careful so she doesn't slip, and I can't say that I blame her, so I go over and help her in. Dad is carrying Sam, which seems weird, but then I notice that she is crying like crazy. I'm kind of embarrassed because I don't know why she is crying. Felicia is carrying my backpack, plus Sam's, plus her own.

Honestly, I never took Sam for being a crybaby. Then Montana tells me why she is crying. I guess what happened is that she tried to follow me up the ladder and the rungs broke and she fell. She didn't hurt herself, but Dad yelled at her and she just kind of freaked out. Poor Dad. My friends keep hurting themselves up here. That can't be good. Probably Dad is worried that their parents will blame him and maybe he will go to jail or something. That would never happen. I want to tell him but I don't. I grin at Sam and say, "It's much warmer inside."

She shrugs and looks embarrassed.

She shouldn't be. I didn't fall and I kind of feel like crying myself.

When we all get inside and the door is closed against the wind, it is almost spookily quiet. Also, it is dark and shadowy. We set to work right away looking for matches to light the candles that are out on the table. I think it was very nice of these people to leave candles out so that they were easy to find! I imagine that if they had packed them all up and taken them home, we would have been in a mess. There are flashlights but none of them have batteries in them because, as I'm sure you know, it is best to take the batteries out of stuff you leave at the cabin so that they don't rot away and corrode and make a big, fat mess.

Once the candles are lit, things are a lot brighter. It is a cute cabin, but pretty damp and moldy-smelling, like it hasn't been used in a long time. Sort of like ours. Right away, Dad sets about opening the flue for the chimney and getting a fire going. We are all still shivering and shivering like we'll never stop. The fire starts crackling and the room gets awfully smoky, so now we are also coughing.

"It just takes a minute before it starts to draw," Dad says. He fidgets around with it a bit more and then *whooosh!* It catches. We all rush over and hold our hands out. Sam isn't crying anymore, but her eyes are all red. Well, I guess all of our eyes are red from the wind.

"This is nice!" says Mr. Taft cheerfully. "What a nice cabin, and look at this!" He points to a sign on the wall that says, *Welcome Friends! Please help yourself to whatever you need, but don't steal our stuff. There is nothing good here for you to find, so don't look. We take the good stuff home in the winter.* It's kind of a funny sign, if you ask me. Are they expecting people to break in? Does this happen often?

"It's like an inn," says Mr. Taft. "The Break-Inn!" Honestly, he is very cheerful for someone who is illegally using someone else's cabin.

"Can we look around?" asks Sam. "I mean, would it be okay if we looked at their books and stuff?"

"Just don't break anything, and put everything back where you found it," Dad says. "I'm going to try to call home." He has a cell phone, which I totally forgot about. Why didn't he call for help? He could have called the Coast Guard and we could have been rescued in that hovercraft thingy. Darn. I guess you can only do that if you are hurt, and we aren't really hurt, just freezing. I can hear the phone beeping, but I guess it doesn't get enough of a signal because of the storm. He looks really sad, but then he says, "I guess what she doesn't know won't worry her!" And he kind of brightens up. I want to talk to Mum, too, but he's right, it wouldn't be good to get her worried and upset.

I can hear Montana and Felicia in the kitchen. I follow the sounds of their voices. The kitchen is not much of a kitchen; it is just a counter and a sink and not much else. There is no stove or anything! How do these people cook? We have a proper propane fridge and stove in our cabin.

"Look!" says Felicia. She is plugging her nose and pointing at the floor. I look, and then I totally scream my head off. It's a dead mouse! There's a dead, rotting mouse in a trap on the floor! Mr. Taft comes running and then he laughs and says, "It's just a dead mouse, girls." He is very calm, and he just picks it up in a piece of old newspaper and opens the door a crack and puts it outside so we don't have to smell it. I mean, gross. We don't get mice in our cabin, I'm sure.

We set about looking in the cupboards for stuff to eat. We are obviously going to have to be here for a few hours and we might get hungry. There isn't much here, but we do find a bunch of cans of meatballs, tuna, stew and spaghetti, which is terrific. I love canned spaghetti. I don't know why. It is totally different from real spaghetti, but much more delicious in my opinion. Our best find, though, is a bag of Ju Jubes. Fantabulous! We start eating these right away. We need our energy to stay warm, right?

Dad finds some cards in the other room, and we set about playing Crazy Eights and then he teaches us to play Hearts. I had heard of Hearts but never played it. I thought it was something super complicated, like Bridge. As it turns out, it is super fun and not very difficult. It's sort of like Rummy, which I am very good at because we play at the cabin all the time. By the time we have finished playing our last round of Hearts, it is dark outside. Or darker, I should say, seeing as it has been pretty dark all afternoon, what with the clouds and blowing snow. Dad and Mr. Taft go outside to check on the weather, which is still raging, and they come back in and say, "We're staying the night!" which is kind of exciting. I figured we would have to. How would we get home in the dark and the blowing snow?

We scramble up the ladder and get some candles lit and try to figure out who will sleep where. There are only two beds up here, just regular size beds, not double beds. There are four kids and two adults! How will this work? Underneath each bed, there are a bunch of sleeping bags in big green garbage bags, which is a huge relief. Well, it's also a huge relief that that was all that was in the bags. After the whole mouse incident in the kitchen, I was kind of worried about what else might be in there. You know what I mean? The bags could have been full of mouse nests for all I knew. We roll them out and inspect them for bugs and they look okay. They aren't beautiful or new, but they'll do.

"The sleeping bags," I say, and slap my forehead. We left them out on the line at our place! They will be totally soaked, if they haven't blown away altogether. Well, there's nothing to be done about that now, I suppose. We just have to worry about tonight. We need these sleeping bags. Even with the fire there is still a chill in the air. Not that

I relish the idea of sleeping in someone else's sleeping bag. That is somewhat disgusting, if you think about it. Who knows who slept in there? Maybe it was someone with cooties. Maybe it was someone disgusting like Tim the Nose Blower, for example. You never know.

At least there are eight sleeping bags, which is fantabulous. Enough for everyone and then some. I'll just have to try not to think about who else has put their sweaty feet in there. I'm going to sleep in at least two layers of clothing to keep all the other person's germs away.

"Found something," Sam says. Which is funny because she is just lying on one of the beds.

"What?" I ask. She points up at the ceiling. Up there, resting on the rafters, there are a bunch of those foam mattress-things that we call foamies. I'm sure they have a more correct name, but I'm also sure I don't know what it is. It doesn't much matter what they are called, we need them and there they are. We set to work pulling them down, and a number of disgusting things fall on our heads, such as dead spiders. My back prickles. I hate spiders. Yuck. I have a comb in my backpack and I comb my hair like mad while the others cover the floor with the mattress-things. It fills up the whole space. Then we put out a sleeping bag on each one, and we're all set for bedtime. The one problem is that there are no pillows, which is weird, but I guess we can use some of our layers of clothes as pillows, such as our sweatshirts or something.

Sam and I are both wearing our Dolphin Diving Club sweatshirts, which are super-nice fluffy ones that will make good pillows. Montana has a thick cotton sweater which she can use, although it will be a bit lumpy, and Felicia is going to use one of her layers of sweatpants. I am so relieved we wore so many layers! Who knew how handy they would be?

While we were getting the beds ready, Dad and Mr. Taft were cooking in a saucepan on top of the fire. I imagine this is how Brother XII and his wife and friends cooked, as there was no electricity then either. The big difference must have been that they used really nice plates and so on. Come to think of it, he must have cooked up those disgusting carrots in this same way. "Hey, Montana," I say. "Take a picture of this for our project!"

She does, and in a way Mr. Taft with his beard and hat looks a bit like Brother XII, so we can use the picture of him stirring the pot over the fire on our display. We will write underneath it *Recreation of Actual Events*, like they do on TV on shows like

Crime Stoppers and so on. I wonder if we will be on *Crime Stoppers* for breaking into this cabin. I forgot for a bit that we weren't supposed to be here. Uh-oh. I push it out of my mind and try to concentrate on dinner.

Mr. Taft serves us each up a big bowl of . . .

"What is it?" says Felicia, dubiously stirring it with her spoon.

"It's *spaghew*," he chuckles.

"Gross!" we yell. "Eeeewwww! What is *that?*"

"I'm teasing!" he says. "I'm kidding. It's spaghetti mixed with stew and meatballs."

I taste it tentatively, and you know what? It tastes okay. I mean, it's no spicy stir-fry or anything, but it's hot and has lots of meat and so forth in it, so goodness knows it is filling. We eat until we are bursting. We don't have anything to drink, so frankly I'm amazed we don't die of thirst, but then Dad comes up with the idea of melting snow in a saucepan to make snow-tea for us. It takes ages to get enough for everyone, but by the time it is done, mmmm-mmm. He found some tea bags in the kitchen, and it is deliciously lemony and hot.

To tell you the truth, I had totally forgotten that it was my birthday, when all of a sudden they all start to sing, "Happy birthday to you, happy birthday to youuuu, happy birthday dear Carrrrrrrly, happy birthday to you!" I almost get a bit choked up because I am so touched. Instead of a birthday cake, I get a chocolate bar which I am not allowed to share because it is my special birthday treat. It is a Caramilk, which is my second favourite. My favourite is Oh Henry! because I like the name, and also because it takes a long time to eat through all the layers. But I'm not one to complain. The Caramilk is perfect.

Wait, it gets better. There is one more surprise! Montana has a gift for me, which was in the pocket of her jacket. The other girls say that their gifts are at home, but I totally don't mind. I mean, I wasn't expecting anything. She passes me a tiny box, which I unwrap — which is difficult because she used about a million pieces of tape. Finally, I get into it and it is a little, pink velvet box, which I open up. It has hinges and it kind of snaps open. I love these little boxes. Inside is a perfect little pair of earrings shaped like dolphins!

"Thank you!" I shout. "I loooove them!"

They are so beautiful that I run right over to her and give her a hug. Honestly, she is so nice. That is why she is my best friend in the world. Not because she got me a gift, but because she knew exactly the perfect gift.

The one problem is that they are for pierced ears and my ears aren't pierced yet, so I guess that settles it. I'm going to do it for sure. Likely, I will faint, like when I stabbed my hand with the pointy part of the compass. That will be a fine to-do. I'm thinking about this and staring into the fire when Sam nudges me.

"Carly," she whispers. "I have to go to the bathroom."

As soon as she says it, I realize that I was just thinking the exact same thing, but one thing this cabin does not have is a bathroom. There is the living room and kitchen down here and just beds and foam mattresses upstairs.

"Dad," I hiss, "Where is the bathroom?" Everyone looks up because I guess we all need to go. That's funny. I wonder where Brother XII went to the bathroom. He might have had fancy plates and cups, but did he have a fancy bathroom? I doubt it. For one thing, how would he have done all the plumbing? I'm not even sure they had proper toilets and whatnot during the time he was alive.

Our cabin is better than this one because it has a bathroom in it, although there is one kind of disgusting thing that Dad has to do, and that is take the toilet tank out once a day and dump it in a big hole. That is fairly grotesque, I'm sure you'll agree. He has a big hole a long way from the cabin that he dumps the sewage into, and he pours in chemicals and so forth so that it doesn't stink. It is the single most disgusting thing about the cabin.

Not that that matters now, because there is no bathroom here, so no one has to empty the tank.

"There must be an outhouse," Dad says. "I'll go look." He puts his jacket back on and thumps out into the cold wind. About an hour later — when, frankly, things are looking desperate — he comes back. "Found it," he says. "Bundle up and follow me!"

It is much more fun outside now that the snow is deep-ish and crunchy, and now that we know we have an *inside* to go back to. Being trapped out here without a cabin to break into would have just been plain scary. We would probably have frozen to death. It's possible. I remember last year some kid got out of her house in the middle of the night and froze to death in a snowbank, only she wasn't dead. They thawed her out, like hours later, and she was totally fine. Apparently that's because she was so small and she froze really fast. I wonder if we are small enough to freeze quick like that. I seriously doubt it.

My ears are nearly ice cubes by the time we get

to the outhouse, which is much too far from the cabin in my opinion. It is also basically just a tiny, rotten, shack-stall thing. I'm sure it is full of spiders and no end of disgusting bugs, but I try not to think about it. By the time we get back to the snuggly little cabin, I can tell you we are all exhausted. We scramble up the ladder and fall into bed, in all our layers and everything. Dad and Mr. Taft stay up for a while talking in quiet voices about how long the storm might last and what they will do. We eavesdrop for a while, but then we end up talking about other stuff. Like Sam says, "I hope we didn't miss anything at diving practice today."

And I say, "I'm sure we didn't. Just the same old stuff."

And she says, "Right. Is Tim your boyfriend?"

I'm like, "What are you talking about? Are you crazy?" Then I start laughing like crazy and Montana and Felicia join in. We laugh so hard I can hardly remember what we were laughing about.

"Settle down!" Dad calls. "Go to sleep now!"

And I guess we do, because I don't remember much more than that except for the rustle of sleeping bags and the start of someone snoring. I'm glad it isn't me. Truly. I can't tell who it is from here, but I think it might be Felicia.

I nestle my head into my sweatshirt and I guess that's it. I'm so tired I can hardly hear the wind and the waves and everything else. I sleep really soundly for a few hours and then I wake up suddenly, and — I'm not kidding — I see a ghost.

I'm sure you think I'm crazy, but I swear it's true. Just standing there, making a weird sort of keening noise, is BROTHER XII. He is staring at me and above his head there is a glowing light — just like he talked about in one of the books! I'm really excited, but also completely terrified. No one else is awake; I can hear their gentle snoring. Well, it isn't really gentle. Dad and Mr. Taft snore like chainsaws. It's near deafening.

The keening noise continues and he/it takes a step towards me and that's when I start to scream my head off because his eyes are all white and scary. Everyone wakes up and the girls are like, "What? What? Where am I?" before they remember that we are in a broken-into cabin in the middle of a snowstorm. Although, come to think of it, there is no sound coming from outside. Actually, it is light outside, which is odd because when I saw the ghost it was dark. I'm completely confused!

"It was just a dream, Carly," Dad says, yawning.

"You scared us all to death."

"So-rry," I say. "It wasn't a dream. I saw a ghost! I swear! He was making a noise, like . . . " I pause. "I don't know. Forget it."

"Did you really see a ghost, Carly?" Montana whispers. "Is this cabin haunted?"

I shrug. No one ever believes me. Well, I know what I saw. And heard. It wasn't a dream! I know that dreams sometimes feel real, but this one was definitely real. I'm positive of it.

"Never mind," I say. "Must have been a dream."

Huh. Like I believe that. It was no dream! I think it was Brother XII and I think if I hadn't screamed, maybe he would have told me where the gold was. Duh. I wish I hadn't screamed. Honestly. I can't stand what a baby I am sometimes. Why do I do stuff like that? Why am I such a scaredy-cat?

We eat some more spaghew for breakfast and then we go outside. It is completely still and quiet and all covered with snow. It looks totally beautiful. There isn't a breath of wind; the water is flat calm. But . . . the boat . . . is gone!

We all stare at the place where the boat was. "Um, Dad," I say. "The boat . . . "

"I see that, Carly," he snaps. Well, really. I was

just trying to help. He doesn't have to be mean. "Oh, crap," he says.

"I guess the storm washed it out to sea," says Mr. Taft, who is more than a little bit calm. How can he be calm? This is a crisis of Biblical proportions! We're trapped! We'll have to live here forever! Or at least until the snow melts.

"Are we trapped?" whispers Montana.

"Uh, no," I say. "I'm sure it'll be fine. It's probably just down there a ways." I point down the beach, where I truly hope to see the silver hull of the boat. The beach does look pretty empty, I must admit.

"I don't see anything," says Sam.

"Great," says Felicia. "I guess we'll just have to stay!"

"Stay!" I say, horrified. "No way! I want to get warm. I want to go home. I want . . . "

"I'll go look for it," Dad says. He kicks at a log and almost falls over. That's pretty funny. Well, not funny-funny, but funny in the way that sometimes when you get angry it backfires and you just end up looking silly. He storms off down the beach, waving over his shoulder at us. We look at each other and head back into the cabin — what else are we going to do? Besides, it's freezing out here. And my pants are damp. And I'm shivering.

"The boat is gone," I say to myself. "The boat is gone. It's an adventure, that's all."

But is it? I mean, it has been so far, but to tell you the honest truth, I am almost tired of adventure at this point. I sort of just want to go home and have Mum run me one of those really smelly hot baths and I want her to pour hot water over my hair and I want to go to sleep in my own bed. The boat being gone is nearly the last straw. I feel the start of tears prickling my eyes so I excuse myself to visit the outhouse. Really. I don't need my friends to see me crying like a baby, now, do I? Especially now that I am eleven and the oldest in the group.

I trudge up to the outhouse in the now nearly knee-deep snow. It is perfect snow for building things, which is good. Later maybe we can build a snowman or something back at our own cabin or maybe even at home. I am in the outhouse, doing my business — well, actually just having a small crying fit — when I hear the keening noise again. Now I know what people mean when they say "my blood ran cold." I'm telling you, every part of me turned to ice.

I mean, I'm not asleep *now*, am I?

I sure stop crying in a fast hurry, I can tell you that. I know this isn't a dream now, for sure. I finish up and peek out of the outhouse. Everything is very still and quiet and the others are all inside. And then . . . I hear it again!

chapter 6

I walk very quickly out of the outhouse and towards the cabin. This sound is very disturbing. I pinch myself very hard to make sure I am not dreaming, and it hurts, so clearly I am awake. I knew I was awake. The thing with bad dreams is that you never ask yourself *during* them if you are actually awake or not. You only do that when you are awake. Also, if this was a dream then I would know what to do, and that would be to scream like crazy until I woke up. Obviously that can't happen now, seeing as I am already awake. I hurry a little bit towards the cabin, concentrating on the door, and then I trip. My heart is beating like mad, and my face is firmly planted in the snow. And I bit my lip, which stings. I am so close that I can hear sounds from inside the cabin of sleeping bags being zipped and that kind of thing. I am just about to call for help . . .

And then I hear it again.

It is a super-high-pitched kind of whine. I take a deep breath and get up on my feet. My hands are seriously shaking. Why am I scared? What could possibly happen? I look around. It is all the same as it was before, snow-covered trees and bushes and a couple of birds swooping across the sky. It is all very calm and lovely. I decide right then and there that I will not be afraid. What a waste of time to be scared of something just because you have never seen it before! What a great opportunity to have a conversation with a ghost! For one thing, I will ask him where the gold is, and for another I will ask him about his religion or whatever because I'm not sure I entirely understand how he convinced all these people to come from all over the world and live here. I mean, I can see why you would want to live here, it's very pretty and beautiful and all that, but I can't see why he was such a big deal and why he thought he was, like, God, or something. Not that I necessarily believe in God. Mum says it's okay that I haven't made up my mind about that yet. It is something I'm going to think about when I am a teenager. Anyway, I asked Mr. Taft about it when we were on the boat coming up here, and he explained that Brother XII started a colony, which was sort of a very small city here on this island, but with no roads or stores or anything, because then the people would not be influenced in any way by radio or TV or stuff in the newspapers because they would be totally isolated. He figured that by isolating them they would be sort of uncontaminated, as though TV was germy or catching. Ha. Obviously, he was a little crazy. But when I said that to Mr. Taft, he said no, that he wasn't crazy necessarily, but just that he believed very strongly in this way of life and that he would be the father to the second coming of Christ. I don't know enough about the first coming of Christ to have an opinion, but it does seem to me that a lot of people on TV and on the bus claim to be the second coming of Christ, but it usually turns out that they are crazy or they are just trying to get people to give them money. I think Brother XII maybe just wanted people to give him money, frankly, and that's how he got the gold. I'm going to ask him. And if he can't answer, if he can only make that very annoying, whining, screechy sound, then I will ask him Yes or No questions and he can nod or shake his ghost head or what have you.

I sit down on a snowy stump — actually the snow is too deep to sit, so I sort of lean on it in a way that I imagine looks relaxed — and I wait for him to reveal himself to me. My heart is going crazy, just like it does when I'm on the platform about to plummet to the pool below. Ha. I mean, when I'm on the platform, about to dive.

Don't be silly, I tell myself firmly. I know that the ghost won't hurt me because the ghosts in books never really hurt people. Also, because I have never seen anything on the news on TV where a ghost hurt someone. I'm sure I'd remember if I had. I close my eyes a bit and listen to my heart. "Okay," I tell myself out loud. "Nothing bad will happen, open your eyes." I open them and look around and everything is still the same. Huh.

"Brother XII!" I whisper. I don't want the others to hear me because they will think that I am a nutter. What other people think is very important to me, but it shouldn't be because Mum is always saying, "It doesn't matter what other people think!" She sounds exasperated when she says it, and she usually only says it when I start a sentence with, "But everyone else . . . "

I hear the sound again. It is quite loud. I could not possibly be imagining it, but it does sound like it's coming from underneath the cabin. Why would a ghost be under the cabin? That is truly weird. If I were a ghost I would float around and stuff. Presumably, ghosts don't need shelter and so on. I go over to the edge of the cabin and there is a bunch of wood and trellis-type stuff so that you can't see underneath. You see, there is no garbage dump or anything on the island, so everyone has to take all their garbage and whatnot home on their boats. Sometimes if you have really big garbage that doesn't smell, like, for example, a couch or an old stove, you don't want to haul that away on your boat because it would be super heavy and you are just throwing it out anyway. So what a lot of people do is put stuff under their cabin. The cabins don't have basements because of the rock. In the city, people blast the rock away, but here they don't bother, they just build their cabin up on stilt-type things and use the space underneath like a big old basement. Anyway, the trellis is sort of hiding the junk under there, and the sound is definitely louder.

I move a broken bit of trellis and say again, "Brother XII!" I'm feeling less scared, particularly if a ghost feels the need to hide underneath a cabin. I mean, think about it. How scary could he possibly be? I crawl under through the gap, but I have to be careful because there might be mousetraps or something under here. There are little drifts of snow that have blown through the trellis, and a few weeds and things. I crawl in a little ways and then I wait. I can hear footsteps right over my head. It is like being at home in the Other Room and hearing people in the kitchen. I feel like tapping the floor to scare them, which would be pretty funny, but I decide to wait. I mean, if I find Brother XII's ghost, they will be plenty scared and they will all think how super-brave I was to find him and ask questions. Also, Mrs. Witless will have to give us a good mark on our project if I have actually interviewed a real ghost.

I am getting less nervous as I sit under here, although I can't believe no one has come looking for me yet. Huh. Clearly, they don't notice when I am not there. I am like the invisible, unpopular girl whom nobody gives valentines to, except geeky boys. How do you like that?

There is an old mooring buoy down here, which is neat, as well as some boxes of nails. I kind of kick the buoy with my foot and it rolls over and hits this big pillowy thing that might be an old chair.

And the sound comes again.

I crawl over there, freaking out only a little bit. Brother XII is probably in the chair. I take a second to gather my thoughts and I peek over the back, and you won't believe what I find . . .

Three little kittens! One of them is meowing like mad, which must have been the weird sound I thought was shrieking. I don't have much experience with cats, so how am I supposed to know what meowing sounds like? We are "dog people," my mum always says. She says the whole world can be divided into "cat people" and "dog people." I'm not sure which one I am, to tell you the truth. I love dogs like mad, but I've never had a cat, so how do I know for sure? The other two kitties are lying very still, and at first I think they might be dead. My hand is trembling like crazy, but I reach out towards the one that is standing, and he kind of backs away from me, staring at me with these huge eyes. All three of them are very tiny and look like they are starving to death.

"Here, kitty, kitty, kitty," I say, and make sort of kissing noises with my mouth. He just looks at me.

"CARLY!" someone yells. I'm so startled that I rise up and crack my head very hard on the floor of the cabin. It hurts a great deal, I have to tell you.

"WHAT!??!?!?" I yell. "Who is that?"

"It's me!" calls Montana. "Where are you?"

"Under the cabin, come here!"

"WHERE?"

"UNDER THE CABIN," I yell at the top of my lungs, which, unfortunately, must scare the little kitten half out of his mind because he leaps straight into the air and darts underneath some boards.

Montana scrambles underneath the broken trellis. It is hard for her to crouch because of her back having to always be straight and so on, so she kind of has to squirm on her belly, which looks quite funny. I giggle and almost forget to look for the cat.

"It wasn't a ghost!" I tell her. "It was kittens. I must have heard them in my dream and turned them into a ghost or something!"

"Kittens!" she says. "Awwww."

She reaches right over and picks up one of the kittens that I thought was dead. It isn't dead. It makes a loud meowing sound and scratches her right on the hand.

"Ouch!" she screams and drops it like a hot potato. I decide to try to pick up the other one, hoping it isn't dead, which would be gross and very sad, to say the least. I pick it up very carefully, making a little clucking noise. It doesn't jump or bite or make any sound, but it does open one eye and look at me. Its eye does not look good. This is not a healthy kitty. It is so tiny in my hands that I can feel its bones and its heart beating madly and all that. I can't believe this! This is better than finding gold, almost. Well, maybe it is. I mean, if we found the treasure, what would we do with it? We would probably have to give it to the police or the museum or something, and newspapers would write stories about us. Well, that would be quite good and fun. But what would be the worst would be that people would hear about it and they would all come here and someone would build a road or whatever and before you know it, this would be just another contaminated city. Huh.

Montana has got the other kitty back in her cupped hands again. It is lying pretty still; I think it might be in shock or something, because that can happen. I know this because once we found some baby birds and one fell out of the nest and it was lying so still we thought it was dead, and then Dad told us it was in shock. "Keep him warm," I tell Montana. This is what you do when someone is in shock, I remember my dad saying.

We need some help to get the third kitten, so it's good that Felicia's face and Sam's face appear at the trellis, and before you know it, they are under here too. It is really very spacious down here. If the people who owned this place wanted to, they could put walls up and make it a proper room. Probably kids would like to sleep here, although adults wouldn't be able to fit.

Felicia and Sam take the kittens and start cooing and oohing and aahing at them. Poor things must be very overwhelmed, I think, but I don't tell them to put the kittens down. Why would I? I'm not the boss. I'm a little worried that they might squish them accidentally or something, though. Should I say something?

No. You're right. None of my business. Montana and I go about the business of getting the third kitten. He is very feisty. First he hides behind the mooring buoy, and then we hear a crash and he has knocked over some bottles that were piled up in a heap. Next thing you know, he has jumped into this old, rotting dinghy they are keeping under here. Why would they have a boat under their cabin? What a waste. It is obviously not seaworthy and it is mostly rotten, but still it could probably be fixed. It is hard to crawl into the boat because there isn't much clearance between it and the cabin floor. By the time I've wiggled in, the kitten has taken off running again.

"Got him!" Montana yells. He is squirming crazily in her hands and then all of a sudden he stops. I scramble out of the boat, getting a million splinters in my hand, and I walk on my knees over to where she is. This is the cutest of all the kittens. He is almost all orange. So cute! Like marmalade or carrots. She passes him over to me and I end up putting him in my jacket and sort of bundling him up because he is scratchy and noisy and not altogether pleased to see me. Though he must be hungry. Doesn't he know I can get him food? "There's tuna in the cabin," I tell him. "You can thank me later."

And we all crawl out into the snow just as Dad appears back at the cabin.

"Oh my good lord," Dad says when he sees us carrying the kittens. "What on earth did you find?"

"Kittens," I tell him. "Can we keep them? Did you find the boat?"

"Carly! I've told you a thousand times not to touch animals you don't know!" He's kind of mad, I can tell. But I forgot! I wasn't thinking about rabies, I was thinking about the kittens and saving them! "I don't think you can keep them," he continues, sighing heavily. "They must belong to someone. And no, I didn't find the boat. No sign of it. Damn it! Sorry. Didn't mean to swear. I mean, darn it."

"Who could possibly own these kittens?" asks

Sam. This is a very good question, I'm sure you'll agree. There is no one around here, that's for sure. It's winter. We are the only people crazy enough to come here in the winter. I think we've already established *that*.

"Um," he says. "Well . . . "

"Maybe someone just left them here," Felicia says, sneezing. Then she sneezes about twenty times in a row while we all stare at her.

"Are you allergic to cats?" Dad asks.

"No!" she says, sneezing again about a million times. It's really quite funny.

"Have you ever had a cat?" Dad asks.

"Yes," she says, "But we had to give it away because my mum's allergic."

"I think you are, too, sweetie," Dad says, and takes the kitten away from her and hands it to Sam. Ohhhhh. It is soooo cute. That one is grey. I think I could love cats. Really. Perhaps I am a "cat person" after all.

"Dad, I really think we are going to have to keep these kittens," I say. "We can advertise in the paper when we get home that we found them or something maybe."

"Maybe someone dumped them from a boat," Mr. Taft says. Honestly, he is quite brilliant. A boat! Of course! We saw a show on TV once about how many animals that aren't wanted get dumped in forests and so on and then they turn wild and eat other animals. The show was about wild dog packs actually, but I'm sure it would be the same for cats. Although, now that I think of it, I've never heard of a wild cat pack. Still, it must be possible.

"Dad, we can't leave them here," I insist. "They'll go wild and maybe when we are here next summer they will be completely untamed. They might attack the baby! That would be awful."

"What are you talking about?" he says.

"I'm talking about leaving these kittens here to go wild," I say.

"She's got a point," says Mr. Taft. "I saw a show once about feral cats."

Ha!

"We'll see," Dad sighs. "Put them here for now." He points at a box. "And pack up your stuff. We have to walk back to the cabin."

"Walk!" I say. "Ugh."

"Don't whine, Carly," he says. "It's the only way."

We go inside and get all our stuff together and make a little thank-you note for the people whose cabin it is. It says, "We enjoyed our stay at the Break-Inn!" and then goes on to explain who we are. Dad leaves them $20 for the food that we ate and writes this big long paragraph about the blizzard. It goes on and on. Really, I don't think they need to know every detail of the story. Also, he offers to pay to get the sleeping bags cleaned, which is very nice of him considering they weren't exactly clean to begin with. Finally, we load up our pockets with Ju Jubes for energy and get our packs on our backs. We lock up the cabin as well as we can, but we don't know what to do about the door. I mean, it's some old-fashioned kind of lock where you have to shut the door and either lock it from inside or lock it from outside with a key. We can't lock it from inside because then someone would be trapped inside. That wouldn't do. And we can't leave it unlocked. That would be crazy.

We stand around for a few minutes playing with the kittens in the box while Dad and Mr. Taft have a big conference about what to do.

While we are playing with the kittens, Felicia wanders off somewhere so she can breathe without sneezing. Poor thing. It must be awful to be allergic to stuff.

"Try this!" I tell her, passing her the metal detector. "See if you can find the treasure, maybe." Well, I do I feel a bit bad that she can't pet the kittens. Also, her eyes are starting to swell up and she's rubbing them like mad. I like her more and more for not complaining. I would have been really upset if I couldn't pet the kittens and I had itchy eyes. I'm a bit of a whiner, I guess. Mum says that I am, anyway. I have to work on that.

Felicia fiddles with the dials and starts trudging around in the snow with it. The snow comes up to her knees in places; it is really unbelievably deep. She wanders around, and gets close to the stump where I was sitting before and it starts to beep.

"What the — " I say, and leave the kittens to run over to where she is. Maybe it's the gold after all. That would be perfect, to find kittens *and* to find gold. That would make it the best birthday weekend ever.

She waves it around the stump. It is definitely something inside the stump that is causing the detector to go crazy. We pass it over the stump a few times until we find the exact right spot. That is at the point where the detector beeps the fastest, obviously. I tell you this because you might not have one of these metal detectors and you might not know how it works. We get to work right away. I help her and we scrape away the snow. The snow is surprisingly heavy and wet. It is about fifteen centimetres deep. Underneath all that, the stump just looks like a stump. We stare at it dubiously. "Maybe it's one of those things like fake books that people have in their house that are actually like a safe or something," Felicia says.

"Maybe," I say, but I'm highly doubtful. I mean, I got a splinter from this thing. If it's fake, it's a very good fake. They thought of everything.

We press on it and pull the little branches but nothing suddenly opens to reveal a treasure. My hands are freezing. I wish I had brought gloves, or even mittens, although everyone knows that mittens are not cool. We are just about to give up when Montana pulls off this piece of bark and underneath it there is a flash of metal.

"It's the KEY!" she says.

The key! Ha ha! It was here all along. Dad and Mr. Taft laugh like crazy, perhaps more than the situation calls for, I think privately. We lock up the cabin and carefully put the key back in the stump and cover it up with snow. It is almost noon by the time each non-allergic kid picks up a kitten, and we set off on our long, long walk.

It is slow going, because the snow is medium deepish and in places very deep. We haven't gone very far and it has been at least an hour of walking. All of us keep tripping and so on because it is impossible to tell what is under the snow. We need snowshoes. Which is absurd in March in the

Pacific Northwest. It hardly ever snows here! I swear it! On one fall I twisted my ankle, and it hurts terrifically, but I won't say anything because I am practising not whining. Also, my legs are killing me. I'm afraid to even look at Montana because she is probably exhausted. The kitten that I'm holding has fallen asleep in my jacket. I can feel him breathing, which is weird and nice. Kind of like a baby. I guess this will be good practice for when the baby is born. You have to hold him really carefully and yet firmly enough so as not to drop him, and if you fall over, you have to lift up your hands to protect him and not worry so much about yourself.

After another million steps or so — and believe me, I'm counting every step — we come to a big bay. This is probably the bay that Brother XII's gang came to for swimming and picnics, I would imagine. Like the bay where we practise our diving. Seeing as everywhere you look on this island there is a beach, the bays become the places that you go to. This one is lovely and much bigger than ours, although instead of proper sand it only has crushed shells and a lot of biggish rocks covered with seaweed and barnacles. You wouldn't want to be barefoot on this beach. I'm not kidding. Your feet would get shredded by barnacles and then poked to death by the crushed shells.

We need to rest, so Dad says we can go sit down on the logs on the beach. There is hardly any snow on the beach itself, which is weird considering how snowy it is in the woods, but Mr. Taft says this is because the water is a "moderator," meaning it is warmer by the water in the winter and cooler in the summer. That's weird, but I'm sure he's right. I'm starting to think that for someone who played golf for a living, he's quite smart. We climb over the logs and stuff and make a little pen for the kittens, who are too weak really to go anywhere anyhow. Even the orange one has mellowed out considerably. I hope he isn't in shock, too.

Mr. Taft gets us to find sticks that are a certain height, and he starts to teach us how to swing them like golf clubs. Felicia is surprisingly good at this, which is funny because she is not very coordinated. She looks very good and Tiger Woods-like, whereas I can't seem to stop swinging it like a bat. Felicia is probably better at it because, frankly, she never could swing a bat very well. We fool around for a little while and then Dad calls Mr. Taft and they have a little secret meeting. I guess they decide that Dad is going to walk on ahead a bit and Mr. Taft will wait with us.

We swing our "clubs" for a little longer, and then

I get bored and wander off. Actually, the only one who keeps practising is Felicia. Maybe this is her "thing," I think. Like mine and Sam's is diving, and Montana's is swimming and violin.

"We could look for the gold," I say. I'm not ready to give up yet, even if the ghost of Brother XII turned out to be a kitten. Although I highly doubt we will be able to find anything under all this snow. We start to hunt around in the edge of the woods and in the little cave-things which are part of the beach. The caves are interesting, but stinky, as otters use them as bathrooms. The dogs love sandstone caves because they like to roll in this junk, so it's a good thing they aren't here. Cats are much cleaner and less inclined to that, I'm sure. Besides, they are all asleep piled one on top of the other. They are so incredibly cute. I don't know what I am going to name mine. I have some good names that I've thought of for the baby, but I don't think I should waste them on the cat. Also, what if Mum says I can't keep him? I don't want to get too attached. If I name him, I'll never be able to give him up. I guess I won't have to worry about it if they don't make it, though. I can hear them breathing from here and it doesn't sound very healthy. I think they need some milk or something pretty quick, so I hope

Dad hurries up and finds us a way home.

The sky is very beautiful and clear today. It all seems like it couldn't be real: all that snow on the ground, and not a cloud in the sky. If it was warm, it would be even weirder; but trust me, it is not warm in any way. I am shivering a bit, and I'm a bit worried because every time I invite friends up to the cabin with me something terrible happens. Goodness knows they will probably never be allowed to come here again!

"Carly, come here!" Montana calls, and I run up to where she is calling me from, which is uphill and it is very hard to run in the snow. I get there — all out of breath — just in time to be pelted with snowballs. We have the biggest snowball fight ever, and we are actually feeling pretty warm and ready to peel off a layer of sweatpants when we hear something!

Putt-putt-putt . . .

It's a boat, and there is a man in it. Wait, it's our boat. The man is Dad! He must have found the boat because he is just coming around the point. I can't believe it. We skid down the snowy hill on our butts, which makes us very wet indeed, but we are too excited to worry about it. The boat looks terrible; it is bashed up within an inch of its life, but it works and that's all I guess we can care about.

"Look what I found up the way!" Dad calls.

"Thank God," says Mr. Taft. He looks totally relieved and I can tell that he must have been pretty worried. I guess things were looking a little bleak. We all pile into the boat, which I guess got carried out in the storm and washed up on the beach last night. We are each cradling a kitten on our laps, and we take off for the cabin. Our cabin. Finally! I can't wait to put on a pair of dry pants. There is nothing worse than being wet and cold. Also, hopefully, we will have time to have some really delicious hot chocolate there before we head back to the big boat and go home.

The little boat cuts through the calm water, leaving a trail of white wake in its path. The seals on the reef all look a bit miffed, as if to say, "What is with all this snow?" Although, of course, there is no actual snow on the reef. I wonder how they stay so warm. They are all lying there as if they don't have a care in the world. Or at least they are until Dad's phone rings and scares us all to death. Half of them flop into the water in fright. I guess now that the storm has cleared off and we are out of the bay, the cell phone signal is stronger.

"Hello?" he says, cutting the engine so that he can hear. The boat bobs around by the reef and a few more seals dive off into the water, staring at us with somewhat annoyed expressions.

I can tell Dad is talking to Mum, and I can pretty much tell what she is saying, mostly because I can hear her from here. It goes something like, "Oh goodness, I was worried SICK, why didn't you CALL? The other girls' mothers were phoning, the blizzard was on the NEWS, I just about called the COAST GUARD, blah, blah, BLAH." And Dad is saying all the right things, such as, "The signal was lost because of the storm, don't worry, we're all fine, everything is just fine, it's as calm as can be, we'll be home in four hours tops."

Phew. Better him than me, I can tell you. When Mum gets mad, she gets super mad.

He hangs up and stares out to sea for a minute.

"Is she furious?" I ask him.

He looks at me for a minute. "Nope," he says. "Just worried. I should have listened to her. After all, she's been coming up here for longer than me, and she did warn me about winter squalls." He shrugs.

"Well," I tell him, "if it's any comfort, it was my most exciting birthday ever!"

"Best birthday party I've ever been to, Mr. Fitz," Sam adds.

"Me, too!" says Montana.

"Me, three!" says Felicia.

Dad shakes his head and laughs. "Well," he says, "best get going!"

The little engine roars back to life, and the island slowly disappears from view.

"Bye, Brother XII!" I call. I don't think anyone heard me over the noise of the engine, but that's okay. I don't know if I wanted them to, after all.

chapter 7

We get home at dinnertime, which is perfect because Mum has made my favourite dinner in the world: hamburgers and fries! It isn't even veggie burger; it is actual burger. Everyone stays for dinner, including Sam's mum and Felicia's dad and Montana's parents. It's so much fun! And for dessert, there is a big, huge cake with my name in icing-sugar rosettes. It is totally beautiful, and also delicious. Before we ate, we all had showers and so forth and now we are all wearing clean, dry clothes. Also, I got to open my other presents. I got: two books, a sweatshirt from Sam that says GDC (for Gold Diggers Club!), a new pair of shoes, a CD from Felicia and a gift certificate to get my ears pierced from Mum, as well as a poster for my new room that I totally love, of Olympic gold medallist Laura Wilkinson doing her platform dive at the Sydney Olympics. But that isn't the best part of the day, either.

The best part is this: Mum says I can keep the kitten! I have decided to name him Treasure, because, after all, that is what I was looking for when I found him. I thought about calling him Carrots, because he is orange, and after all, we did find carrots. Then I thought about calling him Brother XII, but that is really too much of a mouthful, and also seems wrong, like naming your dog Jesus or something. So I settled on Treasure, because he is such a treasure. Awwww. I have picked him up and I'm petting him. Mum says we have to take him to the vet tomorrow to get shots and get him checked out and so on.

Montana is naming her cat Ghost because of how I thought the sound was Brother XII's ghost, and Sam, just to be different, is calling hers Grace because, after all, hers is a girl. Mum kind of laughs and says, "I was thinking of Grace as a name for the baby!"

And I scrunch up my nose at her and shake my head. "Yuck!" I say. Then I see Sam's face and I say, "I mean, yuck for a baby but so cute for a kitten!"

"Are you sure?" she says.

"Totally," I tell her. Honestly. She can be very insecure, which surprises me, considering how brave she is at platform diving.

So Ghost is grey with white bits on his feet, and Grace is mostly just grey. But Treasure is the best of all, because he is pure orange with white feet and a big patch on his chest that is shaped like a heart.

After everyone goes home, Mum pours me one of those great baths, so I can soak in it for an extra long time and warm up all my bones, which are still chilled from the snow. When I'm all clean and warm and between the sheets, Mum brings Treasure in and says that he can sleep in my room. He curls right up in a little box, and when I wake up later I can hear him making little tiny kitty snores. He is the best birthday present ever.

Oh, in case you are interested, I'll tell you about the presentation we did for our class project. I'll tell you how it went. First of all, we did ours last. Everyone else did their project on the Gold Rush, except for Smith and Tim the Nose Blower who thought they were really funny and clever because they did their project about ghosts. For example, they had pictures of the golf course at night where there is supposedly a ghost. And they took pictures at a few tourist attraction-type places that are also said to be haunted. I think they missed the point, because it is not like they were specific ghosts of someone who did something important in history or anything. Okay, I will admit that their presentation did give me goosebumps and I have had to sleep with the light on ever since, but I still think they should have got a lousy mark for not really following instructions. To make matters worse, I was sitting in the front row and Tim the Nose Blower was really nervous, I guess, and he kept spitting as he talked. Smith was blushing like mad, too, so I felt bad for him. It is very weird how all of a sudden they are friends. I mean, they never were before or anything. I don't know if I like them together because they are very loud and obnoxious, which is of course the way Tim the Nose Blower always was, but Smith was quiet and funny. I maybe miss the old Smith a bit, but why should I care? Really. It's not like we were friends.

Anyway, Tim got in trouble at diving the other day for goofing around on the platform and falling instead of diving into the water and, as punishment, we are all not allowed to dive from there for two weeks. Jon said that he could have killed himself because if you hit the water at a really stupid angle it can be just like landing on cement. I think he was exaggerating, but the whole situation was very unpleasant. A tiny part of me is a little bit relieved, though, because now I have two whole weeks before I have to climb that ladder again. I am using my Laura Wilkinson poster as inspiration. I remember at the Olympics, she did this big smile before she dove, and I am trying that. It does sort of relax me, I think. I might look stupid grinning like a monkey when no one can see me, but I don't suppose it matters. I'm practising the smile routine on the springboard because the platform is off-limits. I'm not sure the punishment fits the crime, in this case. I mean, we have to get platform practice in because there are meets coming up soon and we can't not practise. That would be stupid.

Tim is a very stupid boy. I don't know how I ever thought he was cute. Please.

We did our presentation, like I said, on the last day, which was also the last day of March and it was a beautiful day. I was wearing a T-shirt, that's how nice it was. It was hard to even imagine all that snow, but there it was in our pictures. Montana arranged all the photos on the backdrop, and she had scanned in pictures from the books onto the computer and then somehow added them to our pictures, so it looked like the ghost of Brother XII and some other people were there at the cabin with us. It was the neatest thing I ever saw. Then we all took turns talking. We told the class that Brother XII was a religious leader, and that he wanted to teach everyone his beliefs.

"Like at church?" someone interrupted.

"Yes," I said, "like church, but not regular church. It was a different church with different beliefs. They believed in reincarnation and karma and that type of thing."

"What's that?" someone asked.

And I explained that reincarnation was believing that you would come back in another form after you died, and that karma meant that if you did something bad, it would come back to haunt you. "Like for example," I said. "If someone gave you a gift and you made fun of it, you would get bad karma and something bad would happen to you one day as a result." I kind of glared at Tim the Nose Blower for a minute, and then Montana took over. She told the class that all the followers had to give Brother XII everything they owned and he sold everything or whatever and turned all the money into gold, which he hid on the island. Tons and tons of gold! She showed the class the map of the island and they were all excited that it was so close by. I hope they don't all show up there with shovels and metal detectors. I mean, honestly. We shouldn't have said where it was.

So I quickly said, "The followers stopped believing him after a while, because he left and came back with a new wife and she was really mean, so they wanted their money back."

"Right," said Felicia, who read all the books and even found some newspaper articles. "So there was a big court case and Brother XII didn't show up. The judge said the followers should get their money back, but he was long gone, and he destroyed all the cabins when he left." She passed around pictures of the cabin foundations and so on that showed that they were really gone.

I finished it off by saying, "So that is our project. We looked for the gold, but honestly, no one knows if it is there or not, but it seems pretty unlikely that he left it behind. He was crazy, maybe, but not that crazy!" And everyone laughed. We got a really good mark on the project and Mrs. Witless took the china that we found and put it up on the shelf she has at the front of the classroom where she displays extra-good work.

We got an *A*.

And I passed a note to Tim the Nose Blower that said, "Say it, don't spray it!" Ha ha. That'll teach him for being mean to me.

So that was the first real adventure of the Gold Diggers Club. This summer we might have a different club; hopefully, it will be a sleepover club so that I can get out of the house. I think when that baby is born I won't get much sleep! I can't imagine what kind of club we will make up that will have a bigger adventure than our search for the hidden treasure, though. I guess we could keep looking, but I don't think there is any treasure there to be found. Well, there was Treasure, but no treasure. You know what I mean, right?

I'll let you know when my brother/sister is born. I don't know for sure, but I suspect that will be the next big adventure in my life.

Turn the page for a preview of the next book about Carly, *The Actual Total Truth*.

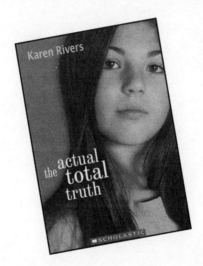

chapter 1

Treasure is lying on my totally empty belly, purring. At least I think he's purring. Maybe it's my stomach grumbling because I'm starving, but I can't be bothered to go find some food, and also if I eat I'll probably grow taller and that's the last thing I need. Anyway, my mood is much too bad for anything that requires moving. It's Very Bad. I don't even know where to start.

Honestly, I don't know what Treasure has to be so happy about. Granted, he's a cat and doesn't know any better, but I feel like he should be able to pick up on my Horrible, Worst Ever Mood and have the good grace to not be so cheerful near me. Or *on* me. How dare he?

I push him off me, which is no small task because he's grown so much in the last three months it's like he's on his way to becoming the Biggest Cat Ever. He leaves a patch of orange fur on my black T-shirt that is impossible to brush off.

I don't know how he does it, but his orange hairs weave into all my clothes like they have little needles on the end and tiny little people sewing them into the fabric. I swear I must stink like a cat at all times. But I love Treasure, even though he is the hairiest, the soon-to-be-biggest and the most orange cat in the world. I found him last February on my island when we were looking for gold. I shouldn't call it *my* island because it isn't *mine,* but my parents have a cabin there, so it's sort of mine. I mean, I'm eleven. It's not like anything is really mine. Except Treasure. And Blue, my dog.

I found three kittens on my island that day (I thought they were the ghost of a crazy old man, but never mind that) and my best friends Sam and Montana kept the other two. They named theirs Grace and Ghost. Both Grace and Ghost are grey, so I'm sure you'll agree that I got the best one, because mine is the most different and everyone knows that being different is better than being the same, unless you are so different that it's just peculiar. It is only fair that I got to choose my kitten first because they were found on my birthday. (I have a third best friend, Felicia, who was there, but she's allergic to cats and so she didn't get one at all.) You have to feel sorry for Felicia for not getting a cat, but at the same time, there were only three cats and four best friends so it really worked out for the best. You do the math, you'll see what I mean.

Not that I'm an expert in math or anything. Math. Huh. Don't get me started.

This ugly carpet is now itching my stomach, but I'm not going to move. It is specifically NOT the chocolate brown carpeting that I picked out for my new bedroom. This is because this is my *old* bedroom, which soon will be converted into a nursery for the New Baby. I go cross-eyed staring at the carpet. If you go cross-eyed and stare at patterns of dots, sometimes you can see other stuff, like sailboats or creepy faces, but that is not the case here.

I swear to you, everything in this house revolves around the New Baby. The New Baby is really going to have it made when he/she shows up. I suppose I'll just sleep in the garage or in the living room or on the front lawn when he/she comes and needs this room. Who knows? It's not like anyone cares. Believe me, when there is a New Baby coming, nothing else matters, including strange-looking not-quite-adolescent girls with troubles of their own.

Big troubles.

To make a long story short, my new, perfect, chosen-by-me bedroom was given to our temporary nanny, Jenny, because of the New Baby. Or rather because my mum was too tired to look after us properly. "Us" being, of course, me (Carly) and my little step-sister Marly (I know it rhymes, okay? Lame. Believe me, this is one of the banes of my existence.) And my littler step-brother Shane. Like we were too much work just because Mum's got a stomach the size of a Volkswagen Beetle (my favourite car, in case you were wondering) and sleeps for fifty hours a day, in between throwing up and complaining. Not that she shouldn't complain. Throwing up is the most disgusting thing in the world. What's grosser? Nothing, that's what.

Why anyone would want to be pregnant is a complete mystery to me, but I guess because I'm my mum's and the other two kids belong to my New Dad, my parents wanted to have one together. You know, like hers, his and *theirs*. What. And *ever.* When they show those *Don't Get Pregnant as a Teenager* movies at school, they should include footage of my mum being sick for the ten-thousandth time and then show the veins on her legs. Seriously. You have no idea. Anyone in their right mind would reconsider having a baby if they got a gander at those lumpy strings, let me tell you.

In the backyard, I can hear the dogs barking, which means that any second now Dad is going to shout at me and make me take them for a walk because my mum is resting and Can't Be Disturbed. (He's not my Real Dad. He died. He's my step-dad who I call Dad because, let's face it, calling someone Step-Dad would be really odd.)

It's only the end of June and the baby's not coming out until July. I guess as it gets ready to hatch, Mum's even sleepier than ever, which is pretty funny. I think she's awake for five minutes a day. Don't tell her, but I sort of miss her. I mean I miss the *old* her, that used to go out jogging and take me to diving and watch my gymnastics practices. I'll kind of be glad when the New Baby is finally here, not because I *care,* but because I'm tired of my mum being Too Tired to do the junk that's important to me, even though it probably isn't very important at all. You know what I mean. For example, she's Too Tired to take me to diving practice or to pick me up so I have to beg rides from friends and I feel like, well, a beggar. Like my diving isn't important to Mum anymore now that there is a New Baby on the way. It's New Baby this, New Baby that around here at all times. Seriously.

Not that I'm bitter.

Okay, so I am.

Bitter-Ella, my friend Montana calls me. Montana is so nice it's sometimes just a tiny bit repulsive. Also, she has beautiful hair, which is black and shiny. She says that she's jealous that I'm going to have a baby to play with, but she doesn't know what it's really like. Trust me. They aren't all cuteness and fun. They cry and barf and need their diapers changed and burp like mad all over you. It's not like they come out and start running around the room playing tag and gooing and gahing in an adorable way or anything. They just lie there, wrinkled and sobbing! My mum made me go to this class at the community centre about dealing with new babies. (Boring.) (And also grosser than I would have thought.) Now that I've taken it, I'm pretty much an expert, and I can tell you that babies are no walk in the park.

Anyway, wait until I win my Olympic gold medal. Just wait for *that*. That will show everyone, especially Mum. She'll be sorry that she was soooo tired and couldn't help me. She'll probably feel pretty bad when I say, "I'd like to thank all my friends' mums for *not* being Too Tired to give me a ride home from diving practice." Not that I *want* her to feel bad. I mean, I am happy about this baby in my own way. (I overheard Dad saying that to Mum the other day. "I'm sure Carly is happy *in her own way*." I like that, because it's true.) Which is to say, I'm not really very happy but I'll get used to it. I got used to having Marly and Shane around, didn't I? I'm not totally mean to them anymore.

I hope.

Not being mean is very, very, very important to me. No one wants to be the mean kid. I want to be the nice kid that everyone likes, like Montana. And also, I want to be famous. Then I want everyone to reminisce about me as a kid and for them to say, "Oh, Carly, she was soooooo nice! If anyone deserves this, she does!" Frankly, I don't think mean people get to be famous as often as nice people. Think about it. Pretend it's the Olympics, okay? Are you going to clap for a mean person or a nice person?

I pull a thread on my ugly old bedspread and half an ugly old flower unravels. Great. I wind the thread around my finger really tightly just to watch the end of my finger turn purple. Once, in Science class, we had to do an experiment with blood so we had to cut off the circulation to our fingertips like that. And then we pronged the end of our fingers with sterilized pins so that blood squirted out. We did tests to see what kind of blood we had. Mine is A positive, which looks like A+ when you write it down.

So, you see, even my blood gets better marks than I do, which is part of the reason why I'm in a No Good, Horrible, Blah Mood. I just found out that my teacher, Mrs. Witless, has called my dad at work and told him that she thinks that I would "benefit" from taking some stupid math class in summer school. Which means a whole bunch of things, like that I'm dumb and a failure and maybe she'll make me repeat Grade Five if I don't take it. I'm so much stupider than everyone else all of a sudden, I can't figure out why. I mean, I shouldn't be dumb. I read a lot. Really, I do. Mum always said that reading makes you smart, so I've read almost all of her old books that she had when she was a girl, and ancient books she kept from her own mum when *she* was a girl. I love them. I love the way they talk in some of those really old books. Oh, man. They say things like "ought" and "shan't." I wish people still talked like that.

Anyway, if I fail Grade Five, my life will be over, I swear. Think about it. I'm already *way* taller than everyone in the class. Freakishly, horribly, dreadfully tall. So if I had to do Grade Five again next year, I'd be like a giant in a land of dwarves. Seriously. It would be way too traumatizing for everyone. I *shan't* do it. So there.

If I have to take this dumb math class then I guess I have to do it. Honestly, I'm very disappointed and shocked and mad. It's going to get in the way of my Summer Holiday, which everyone knows is the whole *point* of life. I mean, everyone else will be outside and having fun and taking tennis lessons and swimming and going to the beach, and I'll be stuck in a stuffy classroom being reminded that I'm too dumb to have the summer off. Frankly, it makes me very angry. I don't know what I'm angry at *specifically,* so don't ask. Maybe I'm angry at God for making me less good at math than other people. Or at Montana for being so smart and getting straight As and saying that she'd be happy to help me with my math. (I mean, that was *nice* of her. See how she's really nice? She would get lots of applause at the Olympics, let me tell you.) But she obviously doesn't know how dumb it makes me feel to have her offer to help me. I *hate* it.

My stomach aches when I start thinking about the Olympics and how everyone in the world would love her and maybe they wouldn't like me as much, but they would refer to me as "that nice Montana's friend." My mum says I worry too much about stuff that is never going to happen, but she doesn't know. How can she predict? Things are always happening. There, a wasp just flew into my window. *Thud.* That was something happening. I should add that I'm allergic to wasp stings, so if it got in I'd have to run around like a monkey with ants in my pants to avoid getting stung.

Anyway, like I mentioned, I'm suddenly very tall. And when I say suddenly, I mean *suddenly.* Like overnight, only that can't be true, but it feels true. All I know is that one day, magically, my pants were all too short (which, believe me, looks dumber than dumb) and I kept falling off the balance beam in gymnastics and hitting my head on stuff. Sometimes I wake up at night crying because my legs ache so much. The doctor said that it is just a Growth Spurt. Then he laughed, like it was the funniest thing in the world. Well,

I'm telling you that being five foot seven in Grade Five is not funny and it makes gymnastics very difficult, not to mention everything else, like trying to not look like the Tallest Person in the World. I used to be very very good at gymnastics. Not as good as I was at diving, but excellent all the same. You know how you can tell you're good at something? When you're doing it and it just feels right. I always knew exactly where my arms and legs and chin and feet were, exactly, even in the air. I can't really explain. But now, suddenly, my body is kooky. I've lost sight of myself. I know it sounds crazy. But my feet are further away than they should be and everything is knocked off balance by my gross, ugly height. Being tall is highly overrated, let me tell you.

In fact, to tell you the truth, I quit gymnastics last week after I fell off the balance beam and hit my head on the edge of the crash pad and scratched my chin on some stupid Velcro that was there for no reason and not even where I expected my chin to land.

I was wounded!

The coach made me get up and do it again. She's very hostile. So I told her I was through — really and truly done with it — and I stomped off. It was just too much. I haven't actually told anyone in my family yet that I've quit, but I'm going to. I mean, I've already decided. I don't even care.

The only thing I really like about gymnastics is the chalk that you get to put on your hands to stop yourself from falling off the bar and stuff, and watching other people flip around. It looks neat. It kind of hurts though. It bruises your hips.

I also liked the way my body felt at home in the gym, but now it doesn't. It feels like someone else's body. I hate it. I don't know what to do about it. I need to shrink. I really, really do. I mean, why isn't there a pill?

What I'm really scared of is that if my freakish height has messed up my gymnastics, maybe it will mess up my diving, too. It hasn't *yet*, but maybe it's just a matter of time. Huh! And that's like my all-time number-one dream — to dive at the Olympics.

To make matters worse (like they could be worse), I didn't get any fatter — just taller — so now I'm all stretched out and gangly. My mum says it's cute and that I look like a model, which just goes to show you that my mum is delusional (which means crazy, in case you don't know). The truth is that I look like Skeletor from the He-Man cartoons that you see on those old rerun channels. I never used to be allowed to watch TV, but now my dad lets me because it "keeps me out of trouble." In other words, it keeps me away from my mum. Well, it's a good thing I've seen the show because now I know who the dumb boys in my class are referring to when they yell, "Hey, Skele-tor, how's the weather up there?"

Mrs. Witless says it's just because they're jealous and *short,* but Mrs. Witless is not exactly a fountain of sparkling knowledge.

My best friends (Sam, Felicia and Montana, of course) say that I look fine and that I'm normal and that they wish they were tall, too. But they are just lying to make me feel better, which is what best friends are required to do. Especially tiny, properly-sized best friends with shiny hair and nice personalities and good grades in Math. All of them. And they are all nice, although I think Sam is more like me, in that sometimes she isn't always thinking the nicest things. Felicia and Montana are freakishly nice. Felicia is shy, too, but Sam is totally not. It's funny that we're all friends. We all look so different and we act totally differently most of the time. Montana is very smart and confident and pretty *and* nice and my most seriously best friend. Felicia is Sam's most seriously best friend even though she's not very athletic the way Sam is. Sam is gangbusters. She's so cool. She says whatever she thinks. Sometimes she gets in trouble at diving though — she talks a *leeetle* too much, if you know what I mean.

Anyway. That pretty much sums it up, then. I guess you can see why I might not be capital-*h* Happy. I'm a dumb, giant string bean with bad balance and a step-sister with a rhyming name who right now is banging on my door, shouting, "Carly! Carly! Come and play tea party!" If only a tea party involved actual food, I'd probably jump at the chance. A foodless tea party with funny-tasting warm water in tiny china cups is approximately the last thing in the world I want to participate in, but I do it anyway, because she's one of the last people in the world who doesn't think of me as a big huge giant dumb freak (except my BFFs, of course). Probably it's only because she's so dumb herself, but I try not to think like that. Really, I'm *trying* to be a nicer person. So I smile at her and I say, "Coming, Mealy," which is sort of my little cute nickname for her. She doesn't mind it. She never complains.

She grabs onto my hand and drags me down the hall to her tiny bedroom, which is, well, not that much bigger than a storage closet. This is because it used to be the walk-in closet in my parents' room, but Dad whacked away at the walls with a hammer for a while and turned it into a tiny room. I'm kind of jealous because I like tiny rooms. When I was smaller, I used to like to sit in my bedroom closet at our old house and read those funny old English books, like The Famous Five and The Secret Seven. If you haven't read them, you should. Really, they were way better than, like, Bobbsey Twins and Sweet Valley whatever.

Her room is cute now. There is pretty cool stuff painted on the walls. On one wall, there is a giant dolphin jumping out of the water and leaving a rainbow. I *love* that dolphin. Also, it must be nice to have your very own bedroom that's not just temporarily yours while you're waiting for your real bedroom to be freed up.

I swallow hard so that I don't start getting mad again. I look for a light, which is an old trick of mine to stop my anger from coming out — if I squint at it long enough, I don't get so mad. It seems to me that I have a lot to be mad about, though. But I make myself smile instead. When you make yourself smile and you're not really happy, it feels weird. I can feel air on my teeth. My cheeks sort of hurt.

When Marly walks, she bobs up and down and her bright red curls bounce around her head like springs. I feel a bit sorry for her. Because even though I didn't get my New Bedroom, my bedroom now is at least large enough to move around in. And even though I didn't get good hair, at least no one calls me Carrot Top, or worse, which I'm sure will plague her throughout her entire school life. Kids are mean sometimes. You have no idea.

We are just sitting down when I hear Dad shouting something from downstairs, so I yell back, "WHAT!" And he yells something else that I can't hear, and the dogs — Roo and Blue — start barking, and Shane, who is three, starts crying. I swear, this is the noisiest house in the world. In the last two months, two of our neighbours have moved away. Coincidence? You decide.

Not that I blame Roo or Blue. Roo is my old dog. She's huge and leaves hair everywhere "with extreme diligence" — that's what Mum says. She thinks Roo makes sure she never lies down in the same place twice just to maximize her hair coverage. Blue's hair doesn't come out. It's blackish-brown and curly. Blue is still practically a puppy. He's very cute. I can hear Dad shouting some more so I put down my tiny teacup of warm water and go to the top of the stairs so I can actually hear what he's hollering. He's shouting, "It's time! We have to go, NOW!" At first I don't know what he means. I'm hoping he means, "IT'S TIME FOR LUNCH." But I know he doesn't, because he never sounds so excited about lunch. Although *I* would be. (It takes a lot of food to grow this much, believe me.) But I look at his face, and I feel my heart drop to the bottom of my shoes and I hug Marly, who starts crying because she sees my mum at the front door and there is a big gross puddle under her, like she's just peed her pants, and her face is as white as a sheet, and all I can think of to do is whisper, "Bye, Mum," and then they are gone.

She's having the baby. It's hatching!

I hear the car squeal a bit at the bottom of the driveway, like they are driving in such a huge hurry they don't even have time to put on the brakes at the bottom of the hill.

I must say, it all makes my heart speed up quite a bit. It's pounding in my chest like it's going to come right out. I wouldn't be surprised if it leapt away and bounced down the stairs like one of those really hard rubber balls that bounce so high they sometimes hit the ceiling, even when you didn't mean them to. Although sometimes it's fun to do that — throw the ball at the ground so hard that it ricochets off the wall and the ceiling and off everything in the room. Unless it breaks something, such as a vase that someone got as a wedding gift. Not that this has ever happened to me.

"I'm scared," says Marly.

"Don't be scared," I tell her. "It just means that the baby in mummy's tummy is going to come out! We should go downstairs and make a *Welcome Home, Baby* sign." I mean, I am just trying to think of things to distract Marly so she doesn't freak out, but the truth is that I am a bit scared myself. I don't really know all of it, but I know it's been a "difficult" pregnancy, whatever that means, and it's all, well, scary. What if the baby comes out wrong? I mean, I don't know what could go wrong, but I could imagine an awful lot of things if I try. Which I try not to do. I mean, it's not like worrying about it is going to help or anything. Besides, people have perfectly normal babies all the time. Look around you! Everyone was once a baby. Everyone once came out. Somehow.

Just then, Jenny — who is our nanny even though I think I'm too old to have a nanny — emerges from downstairs. (Mum tells me to think of her more as a "mother's helper," which is even worse than "nanny" if you ask me.)

"Hey, I have an idea!" she says. "Let's make some *Welcome Home* signs for your mum and the New Baby while we're waiting to hear from them!"

Jenny is very nice and has a handsome boyfriend. I like her. And so I don't tell her that that was already my idea. It doesn't matter, I guess, that I thought of it first. All that matters is that Shane and Marly have something to do so they don't get scared and start wondering exactly how it is that a baby comes out. Believe me, I've thought about it, and all the exit points seem pretty small, if you know what I mean. It can't be anything good.

We pull out our paper and markers and get to work. I stick my tongue between my teeth and concentrate really hard on filling in the *W* that I made, with stars and dots and flowers. It's a big *W*. To tell you the truth, it may be disproportionately big for the sign, but it doesn't matter. I'm just going to make it the most beautiful *W* in the world. Jenny puts some music on and starts singing and dancing with Shane. Marly starts colouring big scribbles in some of the other letters. Outside, it starts to rain really really hard and the sound of the rain hammering on the windows almost drowns out the sound of my heart hammering in my chest.

My hands are turning purple from the ink and Marly is getting bored and starting to do this really annoying whining thing she does where she says, "I'm not whining," in this really whiny voice.

Whoa.

I may not be good at math, but I've already figured out that by the time the baby that mum is having right now is five, I'll be sixteen. I mean, I'll practically be old enough to move out! Which means that virtually the entire time that I'm a kid, I'll be subject to some kind of whiny siblings. Great. To make myself feel better, I go into the kitchen to sneak some cookies and to call Montana. Montana, on top of being the best person in the world and my BFF, has the best phone number. It's almost all 3's, which is my favourite number. I love it when I call her and her mum answers in her funny accent. Montana and her family are from the Philippines. I wish I was from the Philippines. It sounds interesting and exotic, which I'm not. To be honest, sometimes I feel a little green when I think about Montana. My mum says that "green" is the colour that you get when you're jealous. And Montana makes me green. But she's so great, I can't hate her. Last summer, she was in the most terrible, awful, horrible diving-off-the-rocks accident at my summer cabin and she *broke her back*. It was the worst thing in the world you can imagine. Please don't make me talk about it. I will be friends with her forever, no matter what, because it's my fault that she had to quit diving and now has really superior posture because she has a steel rod in her spine. I have bad posture. Big surprise there, huh?

On my way into the kitchen, I stop at the mirror in the hallway to inspect my skin for pimples. I don't have any yet, but I probably will one day. It's not that I want them, I just want to be constantly vigilant in case they appear. I've already started using this blue stuff on my face that stings like the dickens but apparently stops you from getting zits. It makes my face go bright red, but that's okay. It's got to be good for you.

There is nothing worse than zits. There is this odd-looking kid, Smith, in my class at school who is more, um, mature, than the other kids and he has zits. Like he didn't already have terrible luck, what with the weird colouring and white hair. He's funny, though. Sometimes he's nice, which is saying a lot about a boy in Grade Five. Don't even get me started about Tim the Nose Blower who did guess what on the valentine I made for him. Huh. Revolting pig.

I sit down at the table and start chomping hard on a cookie. It's not very good, but I'm so hungry that I don't care. I break half of it off for Blue, who followed me in. Blue stinks, because of the rain. His thick curly hair has a tendency to stink more often than not, frankly. I throw the cookie into the corner of the room just to get him as far away from my nose as possible and I dial Montana's number, which is busy. Haven't they heard of call waiting?

I think about whether to call Sam or Felicia, seeing as they are also my best friends, but not as much as Montana is, and I decide not to. I really *like* them, but sometimes I run out of things to say on the phone and I feel dumb calling for no reason, like I always have to be calling them to invite them over or something. I'm just sitting there thinking about that when the phone rings and nearly scares me to death. I'm so startled that I almost don't answer it, and then I'm glad that I do because it's Montana, and she was trying to call me the whole time.

"My mum went to the hospital!" I tell her, and she's all excited. She knows it's really important to me that my new sister/brother has a cool name, i.e. one that doesn't rhyme with mine, and so she says, "Did they pick a name yet?"

And I say, "No, not yet, they wanted to wait until it was born just to make sure everything is okay." Then for some reason I just burst into tears, which was really an odd thing to do and I'm glad I did it in front of Montana and not someone else who might not understand.

She just says, "It's going to be fine, Carly."

And I say, "I know it is, I'm just, it's just, I don't know. It's just weird."

The call waiting beeps. "I have to go," I tell her. I'm a little relieved, if you must know. It's hard to recover from randomly crying like a baby for no particular reason. It's my dad.

"Well?" I say. "Tell me."

"There's nothing to tell yet," he says. He sounds tired already, like he's been up all night even though he's only been gone for half an hour. "It might be a while."

"I see," I say, even though I don't.

"So I just wanted to call and tell you everything is fine and not to worry."

"Okay," I say, and hang up. I mean, really, that was a bit pointless — why call if you don't have any news? I take the pad and paper which are always beside the telephone and start writing down lists of names that I like. I like names with Zs in them. I like the name Zoë and the name Maizy. Even though Dad says that *maize* is like a

French word for corn, so that would really mean "corny." Okay, so maybe I don't like it that much. But I like Zoe for a girl. For a boy, I keep changing my mind. I told my mum that I liked the name Zane, but that's just because it rhymes with Shane and I wanted her to see how weird and stupid it was to have rhyming names.

Maybe I like the name Jacob. Or Nicholas. Or Max. It's super hard to think of a boy's name and I know I have to work on it because my mum said that I got a vote in the decision. She actually said that I could name the baby, but then she sort of took that back because she has veto power, which essentially means that whatever I pick she can say no to and then just pick something else. Whatever.

I can hear the kids squealing in the other room, which makes me want to go for a walk, so I grab that stinker Blue and put a leash on him and yell at Jenny, "I'm going for a walk!" I leave Roo behind because she is so old that walking is hard for her. There is something wrong with her hips. I always feel bad walking Blue without Roo.

Walking in the rain is weird, because you get soaked, but also because rain prongs into your eyes and it stings a little. For good measure, I do a bit more crying. I'm not sad, but I have a bit of anxiety inside me and crying is good for that, or so my mum says. And besides, crying in the rain doesn't count because no one can see it.

We walk for quite a long time. Blue is not very good at walking on a leash and he keeps crossing in front of me and nearly tripping me and killing me on the sidewalk, which would be a fine kettle of fish. We kind of accidentally dropped out of obedience school early on. There was another dog there that scared the dickens out of me, if you must know. Besides, Blue is very well-behaved if you don't count the part where he can't walk on a leash. I tug on it and growl, "Heeeeeeeel." Like he'll automatically know what "heel" means. It's just that I have enough problems without a sprained ankle or a broken leg.

It's pretty cold and does not feel like the end of June. Next week is the last week of school, and that means that we just go to school and sit around and don't really do anything. One day we're going to the beach and another day we're going to the museum. They're very big on the museum around here and drag us down there at least once or twice a year. It's a neat museum, I must admit. There's lots of cool stuff there. But it's hardly school or important. They should spend more time teaching us dumb math so we don't have to take summer school and less time dragging us around to places we've been a billion and one times and could go to on our own during our summer holidays.

So it's basically summer holidays now and it feels like October. Seriously. It's raining like a bazillion drops per minute and I'm soaked through to the skin. I keep walking because even though I'm wet and cold, at least it's quiet except for the sound of cars occasionally going by and splooshing me with water and the sound of Blue's panting. He's a little bit fat. This is a serious work-out for him. I'm in very good shape so it's no skin off my nose. I start to run a bit to make him work. Exercise is very important, as I'm sure you know. It's much quieter out here than being at home waiting for the phone to ring and listening to whining and crying kids.

Sometimes I think I'll probably never have kids when I grow up. I'll live alone in a beautiful apart-ment and no one will be noisy and bug me. Or maybe I'll have some kids and then get divorced so I only have to deal with them part of the time. That's what it's like for Marly and Shane's mum. She lives in an apartment and the kids go to her place on the weekends now, but not all the time. Every other week, mostly, except when we have them. It must be weird but also nice and peace-ful.

I pass by the school, which is totally empty because it's Sunday. It looks different when it's empty — hollow and scary. I decide to play some hopscotch by myself. I mean, why not? Sure, it's for little kids, but it's not like anyone can see me. Besides, it's fun.

Huh.

Hopscotch, like most things, is significantly less fun when you are alone, is what I find out. For one thing, it's not hard to win. My mum says I'm too competitive, but I can't help it, I like to win things. When there is no one to play against, it's just lame. I should have called Sam or Felicia to see if they wanted to come with me for the walk but they might have laughed at me for hopscotching anyway. Felicia lives very close to the school. I squint through the rain to try to see her house when all of a sudden a rolling gallop of thunder startles me half to death. Blue practically jumps into my arms. Then there is a great big crack, and a giant terrifying snap of lightning strikes down so close to me I swear I can hear a tree sizzle.

Now I'm scared, I don't mind admitting. I start to run for real, which is hard because I keep tripping over the leash and Blue is dragging his heels. Finally, I just let Blue go and figure that he'll follow me. What if I get hit by lightning? Seriously, that is something that would happen to me. That's the kind of luck that I have. By the time I'm in sight of my house, I'm shivering and sweating from running and also completely out of breath. Poor Blue is dragging his leash behind him. He looks like a drowned rat, as my dad would say, not that I'm sure he's ever actually seen a drowned rat or anything. I know I haven't. And how would a drowned rat look any different from a regular wet rat, except for being dead?

I push the front door open and Jenny is standing there with her coat on and the kids are already in the car. "THERE you are!" she says, "You've been ages! Your mum has had the baby and we're on our way to see it! Get in the car, right away!"

So before I even have time to ask what the baby is or if it's okay or anything, I'm whipped into the car and dripping all over the seat as we whiz through the storm towards the hospital on the other side of town.